Palgrave Gothic

Series Editor
Clive Bloom
Middlesex University
London, UK

Dating back to the eighteenth century, the term 'gothic' began as a designation for an artistic movement when British antiquarians became dissatisfied with the taste for all things Italianate. By the twentieth century, the Gothic was a worldwide phenomenon influencing global cinema and the emergent film industries of Japan and Korea. Gothic influences are evident throughout contemporary culture: in detective fiction, television programmes, Cosplay events, fashion catwalks, music styles, musical theatre, ghostly tourism and video games, as well as being constantly reinvented online. It is no longer an antiquarian pursuit but the longest lasting influence in popular culture, reworked and re-experienced by each new generation. This series offers readers the very best in new international research and scholarship on the historical development, cultural meaning and diversity of gothic culture. While covering Gothic origins dating back to the eighteenth century, the *Palgrave Gothic* series also drives exciting new discussions on dystopian, urban and Anthropocene gothic sensibilities emerging in the twenty-first century. The Gothic shows no sign of obsolescence.

Sophie Dungan

Reading the Vegetarian Vampire

palgrave
macmillan

Sophie Dungan 🆔
University of Melbourne
Melbourne, VIC, Australia

ISSN 2634-6214   ISSN 2634-6222   (electronic)
Palgrave Gothic
ISBN 978-3-031-18349-2   ISBN 978-3-031-18350-8   (eBook)
https://doi.org/10.1007/978-3-031-18350-8

Cover illustration: TEK IMAGE/SPL/Getty Images

This Palgrave Macmillan imprint is published by the registered company Springer Nature Switzerland AG.
The registered company address is: Gewerbestrasse 11, 6330 Cham, Switzerland

For Oskar.

ACKNOWLEDGEMENTS

I wish to extend my sincere thanks to my mentor, Peter Otto, who generously made time to read sections of this manuscript, sharing valuable critical contributions along with kind words of support. It has been my utmost pleasure to work with you over the years, and I am deeply grateful for the conversations and counsel shared in your office. Thanks also to Ken Gelder for his critical insights and the many constructive debates about vegetarian vampires. I would also like to thank Dr Josh Bullied, who proofread this manuscript, engaging in lively discussions about all things vegetarianism and vampires that have resulted in inspiring joint academic projects; my friends and colleagues from the University of Melbourne and La Trobe University, for all their support along the way; and all the students that I have been fortunate enough to teach, and whose passion for vegetarian vampires helped fuel my own.

I am extremely grateful to the whole Palgrave team, particularly editors Clive Bloom, Allie Troyanos and Paul Smith Jesudas, for providing me with invaluable editorial assistance. I also thank the anonymous reviewer for their insightful feedback and kind words of support.

Finally, I wish to thank my family and friends for their support and unwavering belief in me during the writing of this book. I am forever grateful to my amazing parents, my aunt Di (and Tinka), my brother Cormac, and my partner Hayden.

CONTENTS

CHAPTER 1

Introduction: Vampires and Vegetarians

Abstract The vampire of folklore, like its offspring in cinematic and literary productions and popular culture, is an undead creature of the night
who drinks, by preference, human blood to survive. However, in the first
decade of the twenty-first century, the vampire's diet was redefined by the
emergence, in Stephenie Meyer's *Twilight* (2005), of the so-called 'vegetarian' vampire, who abstains from consuming human blood. The 'vegetarian' vampire chooses to slake its thirst with animal or synthetic blood
and/or to access human blood in ways that do not harm the human from
which it is drawn. This introductory chapter considers the emergence of
the vegetarian vampire and provides a brief review of the scholarship on
the vampire's changing diet, as well as explaining the focus and organisa-
tion of the rest of the volume.

Keywords Vegetarianism • Vampires • *Twilight* • Animal-blood diet •
Anthropocene

© The Author(s), under exclusive license to Springer Nature   1
Switzerland AG 2022
S. Dungan, *Reading the Vegetarian Vampire*, Palgrave Gothic,
https://doi.org/10.1007/978-3-031-18350-8_1

As Mary Pharr states in *The Blood Is the Life: Vampires in Literature*, hunger, or rather thirst, is 'the linchpin of [the vampire's] undead existence' (93), and what a vampire thirsts for, by preference, is human blood.[1] The vampire's thirst for human blood is long-standing, reported in folklore (Summers, *Vampire in Europe* 117, 218–19, 288–89), speculative histories (Summers, *Vampires and Vampirism* 1–77) and etymologies (Cooper; Summers, *Vampires and Vampirism* 19), and even clinical psychology (Dundes 19). For contemporary readers and audiences, the vampire's predilection for human blood is most commonly affirmed through the array of literary and cinematic vampires whose lust for human blood is their most pervasive and enduring trait.

However, in the first decade of the twenty-first century, the vampire's diet was redefined by the emergence, in Stephenie Meyer's *Twilight* (2005), of the so-called 'vegetarian' vampire.[2] The term 'vegetarian' is used here as a descriptor for vampires who choose to abstain from drinking human blood. Instead, these vampires (the Cullens) consume animal blood, opting for deer, mountain lions, grizzly bears and the like to slake their thirst. To be a vegetarian vampire, in Meyer's sense of the term, is to feed on animal rather than human blood. In *Twilight*, this label is treated as something of a 'joke' (164). As the Cullens are aware, their particular brand of vegetarianism is the 'very antithesis of [vegetarianism's] actual meaning' (Wright 54). Unlike vegetarians of the usual (human) variety, the Cullens kill and consume the blood of animals to survive. However, when the Cullens (and Meyer) use the term, they mean that a diet of animals, and not human blood, is comparable or analogous to a human's vegetarian diet. According to Edward Cullen, subsisting on animal blood is 'like living on tofu and soymilk … it doesn't satiate the hunger—or rather [the] thirst. But it keeps us strong enough to resist'. Edward admits he 'can't be sure' that the analogy is legitimate—he is a vampire, after all,

---

[1] Some vampire legends refer to vampires who sometimes drink milk instead of blood. For further details, see Dundes 20–28. There also exists the phenomenon of psychic vampires who feed on energy, emotions and memories, which dates back to the nineteenth century. For a discussion of psychic vampires, see Auerbach 101–13 and McFarland-Taylor 132–33.

[2] Stephenie Meyer did not invent the phrase 'vegetarian vampire'. It was first coined in *Count Duckula* (1988–93), a British animated comedy/horror television series in which the eponymous character, as the theme song states, 'won't bite beast or man, 'cause he's a vegetarian' (Rosewarne 98). Unlike the Cullens and the other vegetarian (or quasi-vegetarian) vampires considered in this study, Count Duckula has given up animal as well as human blood and feeds instead on carrots.

and even when he was a human, he wasn't a vegetarian, so he cannot be entirely certain what it is like to live off tofu and soymilk (*Twilight* 164). But for Edward and his family (and for Meyer as well), the analogy holds insofar as both animal blood and tofu are substitutes for the primary sources of food that, respectively, vampires and humans are normally thought to depend on. This view accords with Julie Twigg's assertion that vegetarianism requires a person (living or undead) to 'step outside [of] the culturally prescribed forms of eating' (19). In both instances, living and undead disengage from the hegemony of carnonormative and human-blood drinking cultures and seek nourishment from a source lower down the chain of being.

At about the time when *Twilight* was published, a number of other vampire films, television series and novels also appeared which featured variations of the vegetarian vampire.[3] In the long-running television series *The Vampire Diaries* (2009–17), there are vampires who, like the Cullens, subsist on a diet of animal blood. This kind of vampire features in a season two episode of *Supernatural* ('Bloodlust') and *True Blood* (2008–14), where vampires have a newly developed synthetic blood at their disposal that meets all of their nutritional needs. In *The Vampire Diaries* and *True Blood*, other feeding alternatives feature in the form of donated human blood sourced from local hospitals (banked blood) and willing blood donors. In *Legacies* (2018–22), a *Vampire Diaries* spin-off, vampire students who attend the Salvatore School for magical beings are taught to subsist on donated human blood. Vampires who subsist on human blood drawn from blood banks are also found in the British television series *Being Human* (2009), later adapted for the US in 2011, and the film *Only Lovers Left Alive* (2013). Vampires who subsist on variations of synthetic blood are also found in the *Underworld* (2003–16) and *Blade* (1998–2004) film franchises,[4] in *Daybreakers* (2009),[5] in the television series *Ultraviolet* (1998) and *V Wars* (2019), and in Kerrelyn Sparks's *Love at Stake* novels

[3] For the purposes of this book, I describe as vegetarian vampires those who feed on animal, synthetic or donated human blood. Its use in this book, as an umbrella term to refer to vampires who follow diets that do not harm humans, functions as a device to bring the texts I discuss into conversation with each other and, in so doing, to map the relation between recent changes in the vampire's diet and changing social and environmental conditions in the Anthropocene.

[4] See Abbott, *Celluloid Vampires*, Chap. 11, for an in-depth discussion of the re-imagination of blood in the *Underworld* and *Blade* film franchises. See also Stephanou, 124–28.

[5] For a discussion of *Daybreakers*, see McFarland-Taylor 160–61; and Stephanou 124–35.

(2005–14). The vegetarian vampire also appears in Cassandra Clare's widely popular young adult book series, *The Mortal Instruments* (2007–14), which has since been adapted for film (*The Mortal Instruments: The City of Bones* 2014) and television (*Shadowhunters* 2016–19) and Deborah Harkness's historical fantasy *All Souls* novels (2011–14), recently adapted for television (*A Discovery of Witches* 2018–22).[6]

Despite being prevalent in popular culture and playing important roles in the works in which they appear, the vegetarian (or human-blood abstinent) vampire is anomalous. Although in a handful of films, television series and novels some vampires choose to quench their thirst on animal, donated, or synthetic blood, the majority stick to the vampire's conventional diet. The same can be said for the genre as a whole. As Brigid Cherry has pointed out, when texts featuring a 'defanged' vampire—the phrase popular among critics for describing the sympathetic (and often vegetarian) vampire—began to surge, 'horror cinema' often featured 'a more violent and monstrous form of the vampire in films [and television series] such as *30 Days of Night* (2007)', '*Let the Right One In* (2008)' ('Defanging the Vampire' 174), *I Am Legend* (2007), *Thirst* (2009), *Stakeland* (2010), *Priest* (2011), *Fright Night* (2011) and *A Girl Walks Home at Night* (2014) and *The Strain* (2014–17); seen more recently in the television series *The Passage* (2019), *NOS4A2* (2019–20), *Dracula* (2020), *Chapelwaite* (2021), *Midnight Mass* (2021), *Black as Night* (2021) and *Firebite* (2021–). Such works restore 'the edge that once defined [vampires'] monstrosity' (Tenga and Zimmermann 76), which had been softened by the development of articulate, attractive, introspective sympathetic vampires in the 1970s. As Stacey Abbott writes, the vampires of horror cinema and television 'are visually coded as monstrous, often with twisted, deformed or scarred bodies, misshapen skulls and protruding fangs'. They are unable to 'communicate, restricted to feral snarls and growls,' and 'lose their individuality'. This is reflected in the horror vampire's feeding habits: 'When they feed, they brutally rip into flesh to access the blood. There is no intimate seduction, but a violent assault,

---

[6] Monsters that look to animals rather than human bodies for nourishment can also be found in the film adaptation of *Pride and Prejudice and Zombies* (2016), in which pig's brains feature as a dietary alternative to human brains (this alternative is not present in Grahame Smith's novel on which the film is based). This diet stops the devolution from human to zombie and enables the 'unmentionables' (as zombies are called in the film) to retain a degree of humanity not seen in their human-brain-eating counterparts.

often descending upon their victim en masse, like animals' (Abbott, *Undead* 180).

Nevertheless, the introduction of vampires who turn from human blood and choose instead to feed on animal, synthetic or donated blood remains a striking cultural phenomenon, one that this book seeks to address. It focuses on texts that it takes as representative of this popular shift: *Twilight*, *The Vampire Diaries* and *True Blood*; and the novels on which the second and third works are based: L.J. Smith's *The Vampire Diaries* (1991–93) and Charlaine Harris's *The Southern Vampire Mysteries* (2001–13). It also considers Anne Rice's *Interview with the Vampire* (1976) and Joss Whedon's cult television series *Buffy the Vampire Slayer* (1996–2003), two works which include characters that can be seen as precursors of the contemporary vegetarian vampire.

Despite the considerable amount of scholarship on these texts, the introduction of vampires who choose animal, synthetic or donated blood diets is underexplored. Although many critics mention the animal-blood diet in these fictions, they tend to use the diet as a vehicle to discuss other matters. For example, in *The Postmillennial Vampire: Power, Sacrifice and Simulation in True Blood, Twilight and Other Contemporary Narratives*, Susan Chaplin's discussion of the changes in vampiric diets and blood turns quickly to the relationship between vampirism, postmodernism, global and neoliberal regimes of power. She is interested not in the work of diet itself, but in blood's symbolic shift from representing the sacred to embodying neoliberal commodity culture. Others read these works as the products of a post-AIDS world and so describe the genre's move away from human blood as a response to anxieties surrounding blood transmission (Aldana Reyes 56–59; Auerbach 175; Lavigne; Stephanou 125). Still others are critical of the vampire's shift from a diet of human to animal blood (Bacon, 'Eat Me!'; West 2), with some refusing to treat this development seriously (Piatti-Farnell, *Vampire* 10).

The development of vampires who choose animal, synthetic or donated blood diets has also been underexplored in recent studies of the representation of food in Gothic fiction more broadly. For example, in *Consuming Gothic: Food and Horror in Film* (2017) Lorna Piatti-Farnell focuses on cinematic representations of food and of eating food that produce in audiences feelings of disgust, mistrust and fear. However, the examples of '"horrible consumption"' exclude a discussion of 'creatures such as … vampires' (26). Although some of the essays in *Hospitality, Rape and Consent in Vampire Popular Culture: Letting the Wrong One In* (Baker et al., 2017) are interested in the ways in which vampire fiction engages with both human and vampire food and eating rituals, they are preoccupied by the commonplace conflation of vampiric eating with sex. None investigate specifically the figure of the vegetarian vampire.

In criticism that does focus on animal, synthetic or donated blood diets, there is a tendency to link the vampire's changing diet to the genre's late-twentieth-century introduction of a sympathetic vampire. For such critics, the vampire's changed eating habits foreground their growing innocence and humanity (Williamson 41–44; Frank 341), 'moral strength' (Gerhards 242) or 'developed ... conscience' (Tenga and Zimmerman 76), notions characteristic of the sympathetic vampire. Others, like Debra Dudek, place the emphasis elsewhere, on the vampire's emergence as a love interest in contemporary YA fiction. In this 'Beloved cycle'—Dudek's name for the sympathetic sub-genre in which the vampire features as a possible romantic partner—vampires learn 'how to live and love well and how to act [and eat] ethically because of this love' (31). The same point is made by Angela Tenga and Elizabeth Zimmerman, who write that 'by feeding on the same animals that humans eat, [vegetarian vampires] acknowledge human priority' in an effort to gain the 'love [and] approval' of their human counterparts (80, 76). Still others read the vampire's decision to consume animal over human blood as a critique of America's processed foods industry (Fahy 116, 117) and treat their diet as symptomatic of a broader 'repositioning of Goth as peaceful' in reaction to the early twenty-first century, media-generated moral panic and fears associated with the subculture (Spooner 159). When not arguing along these lines, there is another premise, popular with critics, that the vampire's consumption of blood, whether human or animal, in these texts, is an analogy for addiction (Fahy 12, 87–138; Frank 344; Lavoie; McFarland-Taylor 152–55; McMahon-Coleman and Weaver 140–57). Although there is a lot to be learned from these discussions, they nevertheless ignore the significance, with regard to these texts and the genre as a whole, of the vampire's choice to not feed on human blood. At the same time, they are unable to explain why the vegetarian vampire rose to such prominence in the first decade of the twenty-first century—an oversight that is particularly interesting if one agrees with Nina Auerbach's claim that vampires are 'personifications of their age', creatures who 'shape themselves to personal and national moods' (3, 5).

The age in which I grew up and the vegetarian vampire came to prominence is an age of environmental crisis, in which man-made disasters have become more frequent.[7] One thinks, for example, of the Black Saturday bushfires (2009), global warming, the destruction of coral reefs, the death of the Aral Sea (2014), the continuing destruction of the Amazon, the accelerating rate of species extinction and so on. By the beginning of the twenty-first century, 'the global impact of human activities during the last 300 years, [such as] population growth, fossil fuel consumption and greenhouse gas emissions, [were thought to be] so significant in scale that they … constitute[d] a new geological epoch' (Boyd et al., vii), the Anthropocene. In this epoch, 'humanity … [is] positioned as the core driver of planetary change' (McGregor and Houston 3); this 'spell[s] the collapse of the age-old humanist distinction between natural history and human history' (Chakrabarty 201; Zalasiewicz et al. 2009), which in turn 'raises profound questions about how humans should live with one another and non-humans' (McGregor and Houston 4). As Frank Biermann and Eva Lövbrand suggest, the Anthropocene asks us to 'imagine new ways of becoming "human" in connection with the earth and its multiple ecologies' and in so doing 'has become an urgent call to vitalize traditional concepts of ethics, care, and virtue' (2; Boyd et al.; Ellis; Gibson et al.; Haraway 161–62; McGregor and Houston).

The first decade of the twenty-first century also experienced a growing food movement, documented in

> the emergence of "food studies" as a field of scholarship; the rise of "foodie" cultures that both reconfigure and reinforce the relationship between food and social class; the growth of concerns about the industrial food system and its implications in health problems, ecological devastation, and social injustices; and the rising popularity of celebrity chefs, featured on cable television cooking and reality television shows. (Frank 340)

These two contexts—the Anthropocene and the reconceptualisations of food studies—form the backdrop against which this book traces the rise of the vegetarian vampire in popular culture, while also exploring the changing significance of this creature's diet. It argues that these texts, with their vegetarian vampires, explore ways of eating that are less predatory and more sustainable than those based on the consumption of animals. They

---

[7] At this time, texts which mentioned global warming also appeared with greater frequency. Between 2006 and 2009 'more than 40 television, independent, and studio documentary and feature films were released … that explicitly or implicitly reference global warming' (Rust 203).

can therefore be seen as responding to the concerns and questions raised by the Anthropocene: the need to eat, live, and act in better, less destructive ways with other humans as well as non-human actors in our age of ecological crisis.

Reading the Vegetarian Vampire builds on recent scholarship examining representations of the vampire in the Anthropocene. Of particular significance is Sarah McFarland-Taylor's chapter (2019) on the 'eco-pious' vampires found in *Dracula* (2013),[8] *Twilight*, *The Vampire Diaries*, *True Blood* and *Daybreakers*. According to McFarland-Taylor, these vampire fictions, with their changed eating habits and/or sustainable practices offer 'environmental moral critiques of extractivist capitalism and its resource-sucking planetary consequences' (124). In so doing, these fictions demonstrate the power of the popular media system that sustains them to influence audiences to adopt sustainable consuming habits. I deviate from McFarland-Taylor and the emphasis she places on the role of media. Instead, *Reading the Vegetarian Vampire* is focused on the material work that diet does in these fictions to imagine and explore the sorts of human-nonhuman and human-earth relationships that the Anthropocene pushes us to consider. Further, this book identifies vegetarian predecessors in *Interview* and *Buffy*, an important omission in McFarland-Taylor's chapter-long study and criticism more broadly.

This book also adds to growing scholarly interest in the 'much' in texts such as *Dracula* (1897) that tie 'the vampire to the landscape and the environment' (Bacon, *Eco-Vampires* 5)—a connection ignored in recent forays into Gothic fiction such as *Twenty-First-Century Gothic: An Edinburgh Companion* (Wester and Aldana Reyes 2019), *The New Urban Gothic: Global Gothic in the Age of the Anthropocene* (Millette and Heholt 2020) and *The Cambridge History of the Gothic, volume 3, Gothic in the Twentieth and Twenty-First Centuries* (Spooner and Townshend 2021), as well as the essays published to this point in *Gothic Nature Journal: New Directions in Ecohorror and the EcoGothic* (established 2019). As Simon Bacon argues in *Eco-Vampires: The Undead and The Environment* (2020), vampires 'might be a plague on humankind but also the potential saviours and eco-warriors that planet Earth desperately needs' (1). Bacon traces this possibility through a wide range of vampire narratives and films as well as 'more metaphorical examples of otherworldly vampires' (such as bats or

---

[8] For a discussion of the show's eco-credentials, see Bacon *Eco-Vampires* 143–46 and McFarland-Taylor 135–39.

patches of ground that 'control the ecosystem of the surrounding area' and 'require regular human sacrifices'), in which the vampire can be seen as an 'expression of the planet's natural defence system' (8) against earth's main aggressor, humankind. *Eco-Vampires* excludes the texts treated in this study. Nevertheless, as Bacon rightly argues, 'vampires' in all their manifestations 'serve as a timely reminder that to keep both the world and ourselves alive into the future', we must 'accept their challenge to be more at home in the world we live in' (192). In the texts studied here, this work is done in concert with and not against humanity, thereby acknowledging the urgent need to 'make kin' (Haraway 162) with other species in order to curtail climate disaster. This difference is important for the vegetarian vampires found in this study, with their specific 'eco-friendly credentials' (Bacon, *Eco-Vampires* 1) offering a generative lens through which we can view and thereby re-think our relationship with other species and the earth more broadly.

To map these developments, this book proceeds chronologically. Each chapter takes as one of its points of reference the sources of blood available to vampires who either refuse to drink human blood (animal blood, synthetic blood) or at least do not want to harm the humans from whom blood has been drawn (blood bags, banked blood). This enables the book to trace some of the ways in which contemporary vampire television series and novels explore the relationship between species and, in so doing, echoes the concerns and anxieties promoted by the Anthropocene. My approach is informed in large part by the modern practice, politics and ideologies of vegetarianism, which is alert to the importance of the Anthropocene for the animal-other. When used as a lens, vegetarianism creates a framework that is useful for exploring the relationship between species and diet that is at the forefront of these texts.[9] Before proceeding further, a few points regarding the historical practice, politics and ideology of vegetarianism are necessary.

According to the Vegetarian Society, the first formal society of vegetarians founded at Ramsgate in 1847 (Spencer 252), a vegetarian is someone who '[does not] eat fish, meat … chicken', 'insects, stock or fat from

---

[9] Many critics have pointed out that there exists within Anthropocene discourse an inherent tension between humanist and posthumanist thinking with regard to mankind's power over the environment. See, for example, Nimmo 177–78. This book, however, takes its cues from Boyd et al.—and similarly guided by thinkers such as Chakrabarty, Ellis, Gibson et al. and Haraway—who engage with the Anthropocene as a means to rethink human-animal and human-nature relations.

animals' or 'by-products of slaughter' ('What is a Vegetarian?') such as gelatine or animal rennet. There are many reasons for why people adopt this kind of diet, such as the affordability of meat, animal welfare, religion, health, cultural practice (Preece 17) and racial inequality (Foer).[10] In recent years, however, the decision to not eat meat has been driven predominately by ethical and environmental matters (Preece 18). Broadly speaking, ethical vegetarians believe that it is wrong to raise and kill animals for meat. To justify this belief, they draw arguments for why we should not eat animals, which depend in part on notions of animal rights (Shapin 80). Although ethically motivated vegetarians (like most vegetarians) still consume sources of animal protein not derived from slaughter, such as dairy and eggs, it has been argued that ethical vegetarianism, 'with specific regard to debates about species and eating meat',

> amount[s] to a proactive strike … against "the institution of speciesism" by putting into question both the specific placement and the general significance of the border that separates the human from the nonhuman. (Lavin 132)

Speciesism is most obviously at work when we rear animals for food and consume them (Adams; Braidotti 68; Giraud; Joy; Pedersen; Wolfe 7).[11] So by abstaining from meat, ethical vegetarians reject as they rethink (to a certain extent) the traditional human-animal relationship evident each

[10] The history of vegetarianism has been deftly covered in scholarship. For a comprehensive account of vegetarianism's general history, see Preece, *Sins of the Flesh: A History of Vegetarian Thought*; Stuart, *The Bloodless Revolution: A Cultural History of Vegetarianism From 1600 to Modern Times*; and Spencer, *The Heretics Feast: A History of Vegetarianism*. For a focused discussion on American vegetarians, see Iacobbo and Iacobbo, *Vegetarian America: A History*; Shprintzen, *The Vegetarian Crusade: The Rise of an American Reform Movement, 1817–1921*; and Unti. For an excellent overview of British vegetarianism, see Gregory *Of Victorians and Vegetarians: The Vegetarian Movement in Nineteenth-Century Britain*.

[11] Others place the emphasis elsewhere, on the use of animals for medical or scientific experimentation, entertainment and pets. For a discussion of these topics, see Gruen; Ryder 'Speciesism in the Laboratory'; and Tuan. For a broader discussion of speciesism, see Ryder, *Speciesism*; and Singer.

time we consume meat.[12] At the same time, environmentally motivated vegetarians' abstention from meat is also a response to the extensive environmental and ecological degradation caused by the meat industry's operations. This includes, but is not limited to, deforestation, overfishing, loss of topsoil, desertification, ozone depletion and water wastage (Fox 165; Rifkin 1–2).[13] Thus, for the environmentally motivated vegetarian, a meat-free diet is the best way to 'minimize the ecological stresses that are under our species' control' and to lighten 'the exploitative load we place upon the earth's ecosystems' (Fox 167).[14]

Although their primary focus differs, arguments for ethical and environmental vegetarianism share a common ground, namely, the recognition that the way humans interact with other species and, more broadly, with the planet as a whole must change. By rejecting the animal slaughter and suffering that underwrite a meat-based diet, particularly in our age of mass-scale factory farming, ethical vegetarians speak to a relationship of care between humans and nonhuman animals. In their attentiveness to the deleterious impact of the meat industry on the environment, environmentally motivated vegetarians seek ways of living more harmoniously with the planet and other life forms. To the extent that a 'vegetarian outlook [thus] recognizes the importance of ecologically sustainable human activity', just as 'the choice (to go or be vegetarian) also entails compassionate cohabitation with other species and respect for the earth' (Fox 172),

---

[12] Meat, meat-eating and the production of meat have also been linked to practices of racism, colonialism, classism and sexism, as well as poverty in Third World countries. For an insightful discussion of the relationship between meat-eating and sexism, see Adams; Kheel. On the connection between meat-eating and racism, as well as slavery, see Adams 52–55; Harper 155–58; Polish; and Spiegel. For a discussion of the correlation between meat-eating and classism, and meat-eating and poverty, see Stavick; and Nibert, respectively. See also Mayes, Chaps. 1 and 2; Ogle; and Rifkin, part one and two, for excellent accounts of the part that the cattle and sheep industries have played in the dispossession of Indigenous cultures by white settlers throughout history.

[13] See, in particular, Rifkin, part five, for an extensive analysis of the environmental toll of our beef consumption.

[14] While this may be true of meat-eating, sustainability discourse also points to the adverse environmental impact of a Western vegetarian diet through the production and overconsumption of foods such as quinoa, as well as soy or almond milks: the former as it relates to food insecurity in developing nations in which they are predominantly grown, and the latter two's links to deforestation in Brazil and desertification in California respectively. Not dissimilarly, sustainability discourse is alert to reasons as to why people do not adopt a vegetarian or plant-based diet because of cultural, religious, health and accessibility concerns (food apartheid).

vegetarianism offers a generative lens through which we can view and thereby re-think our relationship with other species and the earth more broadly.[15]

The examples of North American vampire fiction discussed in the following pages can be read as exploring, through the lenses offered by various depictions of relations between humans and vampires, how to best live and eat, and how best to interact with other species, in the Anthropocene. Almost all the essential relationships in these texts are between humans and vampires, with (some) vampires emerging as helpers and protectors of humanity, with the capacity to become friends, lovers and even family to the humans they meet. This intimacy can be seen as responding to the changing social and environmental needs and concerns raised by the Anthropocene. Chapter 2 begins in the late-twentieth century with an examination of Anne Rice's *Interview with the Vampire*. In this novel we encounter, for the first time in vampire fiction, a human-blood-abstinent vampire. Although Louis subsists on animal blood only for a short period of time, his diet marks the inaugural moment in which a vampire can *choose* to consume blood that has not been drawn from humans. As this chapter will argue, this makes possible a range of future developments in vampire fiction, such as the vegetarian vampire. We can therefore view Louis's non-traditional (for vampires, at this time) animal-blood diet as anticipating, making possible, and influencing key developments in later vampire fiction. It is those aspects of the text that make this influence possible that this chapter sets out to explore.

Chapter 3 traces the next stage in the emergence of the vegetarian vampire, as seen in Joss Whedon's *Buffy the Vampire Slayer*. This series features not one but two human-blood-abstinent vampires, along with some key developments, which are made possible by an animal-blood diet, that anticipate the inter-species relationships later seen in *Mysteries* and *True Blood*. It is important to add, however, that nothing is simple in *Buffy*— certainly not its treatment of vampiric diets. As this chapter will argue, although *Buffy* takes some important steps forward in the portrayal of relations between species (human-vampire), made possible by the adoption by vampires of an animal-blood diet, further steps are not taken, owing to the primal antagonism between vampires and slayers that

---

[15]For an opposing view on a number of issues in this section related to vegetarianism's power to re-think human-animal relations, see Plumwood.

structures the narrative as a whole and so conditions its depiction of human-vampire relations.

Chapter 4, Vegetarian Vampires: *Twilight*, Sustainability and Salvation, turns to Stephenie Meyer's *Twilight* saga, which develops what could be called a 'green' (McFarland-Taylor 2, 144) take on vampiric vegetarianism, one that is highly attuned to vegetarianism's modern concerns and conditions. As noted earlier, modern vegetarianism is guided in large part by concerns for animal welfare and by the environmental damage caused by a meat-based diet. Both concerns inflect Meyer's description of the Cullens' vegetarian practice, which is guided not only by a desire to protect humans (a recognition of their right to not be fed on) but also by environmental considerations. Arguably, it is here, in *Twilight*, that vampire fiction begins overtly to engage with the material concerns and conditions of the Anthropocene.

Chapters 5 and 6 continue the line of enquiry begun in the fourth chapter, namely, that the dietary shift in contemporary vampire fiction to animal or synthetic blood is best understood as a response to the Anthropocene. Where previous chapters have focused on, respectively, a single text, a television series, and a book series, in Chaps. 5 and 6, a book series is compared with its later television adaptation. Chapter 5 places the long-running television series *The Vampire Diaries* in dialogue with the book series on which it is based, written by L.J. Smith. As this chapter will argue, in its depiction of vampiric diets, the television series deviates substantially from its source material. In these deviations, the television series takes up the Cullens' call to explore more sustainable, less exploitative ways of living with other-than-human actors on this more-than-human earth. Of particular importance to this chapter is the television series' introduction of donated human blood drawn from hospital blood bags to the vampire's menu. Much is made of this diet in the television series, where it is presented as a non-violent and potentially more ethical source of blood than animals (no humans or animals were killed or hurt in the extraction of this blood). Therefore, in the context of the Anthropocene, the television series presents donated human blood as another sustainable as well as ethical source of nourishment for vampires.

Whereas Chaps 2, 3 and 4 focus on animal-blood drinking vampires and the fifth on sustainable sources of human blood, Chap 6 turns to texts in which vampires have available to them synthetic blood, namely, Charlaine Harris's *The Southern Vampire Mysteries* and its television adaptation, *True Blood*. This commodity, manufactured in Japanese labs and marketed to vampires as True Blood, expands still further the possibilities for human-vampire relations while making it possible for the vegetarian vampire, discussed in earlier chapters, to become vegan. However, *Mysteries* and *True Blood* represent in very different ways the possibilities that these developments open for inter-species relations. The first half of this chapter focuses on the *Mysteries* novels, which are optimistic about the possibility of inter-species relations opened by synthetic blood. In contrast, *True Blood* brings to the fore the societal tensions inflamed by inter-species relations, caused by prejudice, racism and speciesism, which in *Mysteries* are largely left in the background. *True Blood* illustrates, therefore, the difficulties that lie in wait for the new world made possible by vampires turning to a vegetarian or vegan diet. It suggests that there are issues at the level of humanity that must be addressed before mankind can be capable of a 'greater moral-ethical response, and responsibility, to non-human [and inhuman] life forms' (Nayar 8).

The book's concluding chapter focuses on the recent surge or, perhaps, resurgence of texts in which the vampire's monstrous thirst for human blood is not diminished. It argues that this strand of the vampire story, at the point of feeding, complements rather than dispatches the developments and concerns of the vegetarian vampire. It demonstrates this with reference to recent literary and cinematic productions in which the vampire is linked to fears of viral contagion, voracious consumption and bio-threats—fears that are linked to the vampire's feeding practices, which in these texts are the vehicles of contagion, but also to the collapse of the boundaries that have traditionally divided self and other, human and non-human, nature and culture. In other words, this strand of the vampire story can be seen as anxious about and responsive to our growing awareness of how inter-connected and enmeshed we are with nonhuman and inhuman life forms. If the vegetarian vampire speaks to the need to extend 'traditional concepts of ethics, care, and virtue' (Biermann and Lövbrand 2) to animals and the earth, the vampire as virus can be seen as evoking in fictional form the disaster in store if we are unable to adopt more mindful eating practices and the growing recognition that the boundary between humans and animals is not as impermeable as was once thought.

When seen as a whole, the narratives discussed in this book, with their vegetarian and now vegan vampires, speak to many of the concerns that have arisen in the Anthropocene. Nina Auerbach claims that each generation of vampires 'feeds on his age distinctively because he embodies that age' (1). But as this book will show, it is *how* the vampire feeds that speaks to the social and environmental conditions of our own times.

WORKS CITED

Abbott, Stacey. *Celluloid Vampires: Life After Death in the Modern World*. Texas UP, 2007. *JSTOR*, www.jstor.org/stable/10.7560/716957.
———. *Undead Apocalypse: Vampires and Zombies in the 21st Century*. Edinburgh UP, 2016. *JSTOR*, www.jstor.org/stable/10.3366/j.ctt1g050nn.
Adams, Carol. *The Sexual Politics of Meat: A Feminist-Vegetarian Critical Theory*. 20th anniversary ed., Continuum, 2010.
Aldana Reyes, Xavier. '"Who Ordered the Hamburger with AIDS?": Haematophilic Semiotics in *Tru(e) Blood*.' *Gothic Studies*, vol. 15, no. 1, May 2013, pp. 55–65. *Edinburgh UP*, https://doi.org/10.7227/GS.15.1.6.
Auerbach, Nina. *Our Vampires, Ourselves*. Chicago UP, 1995.
Bacon, Simon. 'Eat Me! The Morality of Hunger in Vampiric Cuisine.' *Images of the Modern Vampire: The Hip and the Atavistic*, edited by Barbara Brodman and James E. Doan, Farleigh Dickinson UP, 2013, pp. 41–51. *ProQuest Ebook Central*, ebookcentral.proquest.com/lib/unimelb/detail.action?docID= 1466965.
———. *Eco-Vampires:* The Undead and the Environment. McFarland, 2020.
Baker, David, et al., editors. *Hospitality, Rape and Consent in Vampire Popular Culture: Letting the Wrong One In*. Palgrave Macmillan, 2017.
Biermann, Frank, and Eva Lövbrand. Introduction. 'Encountering the Anthropocene: Setting the Scene.' *Anthropocene Encounters: New Directions in Green Political Thinking*, edited by Frank Biermann and Eva Lövbrand, Cambridge UP, 2019, pp. 1–22. *Cambridge Core*, https://doi.org/10.1017/9781108646673.
Boyd, Madeleine, et al. Introduction. The Human Animal Research, pp. vii–xxiv.
Braidotti, Rosi. *The Posthuman*. Polity Press, 2013.
Chakrabarty, Dipesh. 'The Climate of History: Four Theses.' *Critical Inquiry*, vol. 35, no. 2, winter 2009, pp. 197–222. *JSTOR*, www.jstor.org/stable/10.1086/596640.
Chaplin, Susan. *The Postmillennial Vampire: Power, Sacrifice and Simulation in True Blood, Twilight and Other Contemporary Narratives*. Palgrave Pivot, 2017. *Springer Link*, https://doi.org/10.1007/978-3-319-48372-6.
Cherry, Brigid. 'Defanging the Vampire: Projected Interactivity and All Human *Twilight* Fan-fic.' *Screening Twilight: Critical Approaches to a Cinematic Phenomenon*, edited by Wickham Clayton, and Sarah Harman, I.B. Tauris, 2014, pp. 173–86.
Clare, Cassandra. *The Mortal Instruments: The City of Bones*. Simon and Schuster, 2007.

Cooper, Brian. 'The Word "Vampire": Its Slavonic Form and Origin.' *Journal of Slavic Linguistics*, vol. 13, no. 2, summer-fall 2005, pp. 251–70. *JSTOR*, www.jstor.org/stable/24599658.

Dudek, Debra. *The Beloved Does Not Bite: Moral Vampires and the Humans Who Love Them*. Routledge, 2018. *Taylor and Francis Online*, https://doi.org/10.4324/9781315225425.

Dundes, Alan. 'The Vampire As Bloodthirsty Revenant: A Psychoanalytic Postmortem.' *Bloody Mary in the Mirror: Essays in Psychoanalytic Folkloristics*. Mississippi UP, 2002, pp. 16–32. *JSTOR*, www.jstor.org/stable/j.ctt2tvfn2.

Ellis, Erle C. *Anthropocene: A Very Short Introduction*. Oxford UP, 2018, https://doi.org/10.1093/actrade/9780198792987.001.0001.

Fahy, Thomas. *Dining with Madmen: Fat, Food, and the Environment in 1980s Horror*. Mississippi UP, 2019.

Foer, Jonathan Safran. 'The End of Meat Is Here.' *The New York Times*, 21 May 2020, www.nytimes.com/2020/05/21/opinion/coronavirus-meat-vegetarianism.html. Accessed 25 May 2020.

Fox, Michael Allen. 'Vegetarianism and Planetary Health.' *Ethics and Environments*, vol. 5, no. 2, autumn 2000, pp. 163–74.

Frank, Alexandra C. 'All-Consuming Passions: Vampire Foodways in Contemporary Film and Television.' *What's Eating You? Food and Horror on Screen*, edited by Cynthia J. Miller et al., Bloomsbury Academic, 2017, pp. 339–52.

Gerhards, Lea. 'Vampires "On a Special Diet": Identity and the Body in Contemporary Media Texts.' *Dracula and the Gothic in Literature, Pop Culture and the Arts*, edited by Isabel Ermida, BRILL, 2015, pp. 237–58. *ProQuest Ebook Central*, ebookcentral.proquest.com/lib/unimelb/detail.action?docID=4007474.

Gibson, Katherine, et al. Preface. *Manifesto for Living in the Anthropocene*, edited by Katherine Gibson et al., Punctum Books, 2015, pp. v–viii. *Open Access*, http://library.oapen.org/handle/20.500.12657/25521.

Giraud, Eva. 'Veganism as Affirmative Biopolitics: Moving Towards a Posthumanist Ethics?' *PhaenEx: Journal of Existential and Phenomenological Theory and Culture*, vol. 8, no. 2, pp. 47–79, https://doi.org/10.22329/p.v8i2.4087.

Gregory, James. *Of Victorians and Vegetarians: The Vegetarian Movement in Nineteenth Century Britain*. I.B. Tauris, 2007. ProQuest Ebook Central, ebookcentral.proquest.com/lib/unimelb/detail.action?docID=676762.

Gruen, Lori. 'Dismantling Oppression: An Analysis of the Connection Between Women and Animals.' *Ecofeminism: Women, Animals, Nature*, edited by Greta Gaard, Temple UP, 1993, pp. 60–90. *JSTOR*, www.jstor.org/stable/j.ctt14bt5pf.

Haraway, Donna. 'Anthropocene, Capitalocene, Plantationocene, Chthulucene: Making Kin.' *Environmental Humanities*, vol. 6, no.1, 2015, pp. 159–65, environmentalhumanities.org/arch/vol6/6.7.pdf.

Harkness, Deborah. *The Book of Life*. Viking, 2014.
———. *A Discovery of Witches*. Viking, 2011.
———. *Shadow of Night*. Viking, 2012.
Harper, A. Breeze. *Sistah Vegan: Black Female Vegans Speak on Food, Identity, Health, and Society*. Lantern Books, 2009.
The Human Animal Research, editors. *Animals in the Anthropocene: Critical perspectives on non-human futures*. Sydney UP, 2015. *JSTOR*, https://www.jstor.org/stable/j.ctt1bh4b7h.
Iacobbo, Karen, and Michael Iacobbo. *Vegetarian America: A History*. Praeger, 2004.
Joy, Melanie. *Why We Love Dogs, Eat Pigs and Wear Cows: An Introduction to Carnism*. Conari Press, 2011.
Kalof, Linda, and Amy Fitzgerald, editors. *The Animals Reader: The Essential Classic and Contemporary Writings*. Oberg, 2007.
Kheel, Marti. 'The Killing Game: An Ecofeminist Critique of Hunting.' *Journal of the Philosophy of Sport*, vol. 23, no. 1, 1996, pp. 30–44. *Taylor and Francis Online*, https://doi.org/10.1080/00948705.1996.9714529.
Lavigne, Carlen. 'Sex, Blood and (Un)Death: The Queer Vampire and HIV.' *Journal of Dracula Studies*, vol. 6, 2004, pp. 1–9, research.library.kutztown.edu/dracula-studies/vol6/iss1/4/.
Lavin, Chad. *Eating Anxiety: The Perils of Food Politics*. Minnesota UP, 2013.
Lavoie, Dusty. 'The Vampires of *True Blood* and Beyond: Bodies, Desires, and Addictions in the Social Imaginary.' *The Body in Culture and Society*, special issue of *Proteus: A Journal of Ideas*, vol. 28, no. 1, spring 2012, pp. 29–36, www.ship.edu/globalassets/proteus/2012proteus204.pdf.
Mayes, Christopher. *Unsettling Food Politics: Agriculture, Dispossession and Sovereignty in Australia*. Rowman and Littlefield International, 2018. *ProQuest Ebook Central*, ebookcentral.proquest.com/lib/unimelb/detail.action?docID=5497698.
McFarland-Taylor, Sarah. *Ecopiety: Green Media and the Dilemma of Environmental Virtue*. NYU Press, 2019.
McGregor, Andrew, and Donna Houston. 'Cattle in the Anthropocene: Four Propositions.' *Transactions of the Institute of British Geographers*, vol. 43, no. 1, Mar. 2018, pp. 3–16. *EBSCOhost*, https://doi.org/10.1111/tran.12193.
McMahon-Coleman, Kimberly, and Roslyn Weaver. *Werewolves and Other Shapeshifters in Popular Culture: A Thematic Analysis of Recent Depictions*. McFarland, 2012. *ProQuest Ebook Central*, ebookcentral.proquest.com/lib/unimelb/detail.action?docID=928922.
Meyer, Stephenie. *Twilight*. Little, Brown, 2005.
Millette, Holly-Gale, and Ruth Heholt. *The New Urban Gothic: Global Gothic in the Age of the Anthropocene*. Palgrave Macmillan, 2020.
Nayar, Pramod K. *Posthumanism*. Polity, 2014.

Nibert, David. 'The Promotion of "Meat" and Its Consequences.' Kalof and Fitzgerald, pp. 182–89.

Nimmo, Richie. 'Apiculture in the Anthropocene: Between Posthumanism and Critical Animal Studies.' The Human Animal Research, pp. 177–200.

Ogle, Maureen. *In Meat We Trust: An Unexpected History of Carnivore America.* Houghton Mifflin Harcourt, 2013.

Pedersen, Helena. 'Release the Moths: Critical Animal Studies and the Posthumanist Impulse.' *Culture, Theory, and Critique*, vol. 52, no. 1, Apr. 2011, pp. 65–81. *Taylor and Francis Online*, https://doi.org/10.108 0/14735784.2011.621663.

Pharr, Mary. 'Vampiric Appetite in *I Am Legend, Salem's Lot* and *The Hunger*.' *The Blood Is the Life: Vampires in Literature*, edited by Leonard G. Heldreth and Mary Pharr, Bowling Green State UP, 1999, pp. 93–103.

Piatti-Farnell, Lorna. *Consuming Gothic: Food and Horror in Film.* Palgrave Macmillan, 2017.

———. *The Vampire in Contemporary Popular Literature.* Routledge, 2014.

Plumwood, Val. 'Animals and Ecology: Towards a Better Integration.' *The Eye of the Crocodile*, edited by Lorraine Shannon, ANU Press, 2012, pp. 77–90. *JSTOR*, www.jstor.org/stable/j.ctt24hcd2.

Polish, Jennifer. 'Decolonizing Veganism: On Resisting Vegan Whiteness and Racism.' *Critical Perspectives on Veganism*, edited by Jodey Castricano and Rasmus R. Simonsen, Palgrave Macmillan, 2016, pp. 373–91. *Springer Link*, https://doi.org/10.1007/978-3-319-33419-6.

Preece, Rod. *Sins of the Flesh: A History of Vegetarian Thought.* UBC Press, 2008. *ProQuest Ebook Central*, ebookcentral.proquest.com/lib/unimelb/detail. action?docID=3412608.

Rice, Anne. *Interview with the Vampire.* 1976. Sphere, 2008.

Rifkin, Jeremy. *Beyond Beef: The Rise and Fall of the Cattle Culture.* Dutton, 1992.

Rosewarne, Lauren. *American Taboo: The Forbidden Words, Unspoken Rules, and Secret Morality of Popular Culture.* ABC-CLIO, LLC, 2013. *ProQuest Ebook Central*, ebookcentral.proquest.com/lib/unimelb/detail.action?docID= 1495769.

Rust, Stephen. 'Hollywood and Climate Change.' *Ecocinema Theory and Practice*, edited by Stephen Rust et al., Routledge, 2012, pp. 191–212. *ProQuest Ebook Central*, ebookcentral.proquest.com/lib/unimelb/detail.action?docID= 1024590.

Ryder, Richard D. 'Speciesism in the Laboratory.' Singer, pp. 109–27.

———. *Speciesism, Painism and Happiness: A Morality for the Twenty-First Century.* Andrews UK Ltd., 2011. *ProQuest Ebook Central*, ebookcentral.pro-quest.com/lib/unimelb/detail.action?docID=4393861.

Shapin, Steven. 'Vegetable Love.' *The New Yorker*, 22 Jan. 2007, www.newyorker. com/magazine/2007/01/22/vegetable-love. Accessed 25 Mar. 2018.

Shprintzen, Adam D. *The Vegetarian Crusade: The Rise of an American Reform Movement, 1817–1921*. North Carolina UP, 2013. *JSTOR*, https://doi.org/10.5149/9781469608921_shprintzen.

Singer, Peter, editor. *In Defense of Animals: The Second Wave*. Wiley, 2013. *ProQuest Ebook Central*, ebookcentral.proquest.com/lib/unimelb/reader.action?docID=707840.

Sparks, Kerrelyn. *Vampes in the City*. Avon, 2006.

———. *Secret Life of a Vampire*. Avon, 2009.

Spencer, Collin. *The Heretics Feast: A History of Vegetarianism*. Fourth Estate, 1993.

Spiegel, Marjorie. *The Dreaded Comparison: Human and Animal Slavery*. Mirror Books, 1996.

Spooner, Catherine. 'Gothic Charm School; or, How Vampires Learned to Sparkle.' *Open Graves, Open Minds: Representations of Vampires and the Undead from the Enlightenment to the Present Day*, edited by Sam George and Bill Hughes, Manchester UP, 2013, pp. 146–64. *JSTOR*, www.jstor.org/stable/j.ctt18mvm36.15.

Spooner, Catherine, and Dale Hudson, editors. *The Cambridge History of the Gothic: Gothic in the Twentieth and Twenty-First Centuries*. Vol. 3, Cambridge UP, 2021.

Stavick, J.E.D. 'Love at First Beet: Vegetarian Critical Theory Meets *Dracula*.' *Victorian Newsletter*, vol. 89, spring 1996, pp. 23–9.

Stephanou, Aspasia. *Reading Vampire Gothic Through Blood: Bloodlines*. Palgrave Macmillan, 2014. *ProQuest Ebook Central*, ebookcentral.proquest.com/lib/unimelb/detail.action?docID=1765631.

Stoker, Bram. *Dracula*. Rev. ed., Penguin Group, 2003.

Stuart, Tristram. *The Bloodless Revolution: A Cultural History of Vegetarianism from 1600 to Modern Times*. W.W. Norton and Company, 2008.

Summers, Montague. *The Vampire in Europe*. 2003. Routledge, 2011. *ProQuest Ebook Central*, ebookcentral.proquest.com/lib/unimelb/detail.action?docID=1655769.

———. *The Vampire in Legend and Lore*. Dover Publishing Inc, 2001.

Tenga, Angela, and Elizabeth Zimmerman, 'Vampire Gentlemen and Zombie Beasts: A Rendering of True Monstrosity.' *Gothic Studies*, vol. 15, no. 1, May 2013, pp. 76–87. *Edinburgh UP*, https://doi.org/10.7227/GS.15.1.8.

Tuan, Yi-Fu. 'Animal Pets: Cruelty and Affection.' Kalof and Fitzgerald, pp. 141–53.

Twigg, Julie. 'Vegetarianism and the Meanings of Meat.' *The Sociology of Food and Eating*, edited by Anne Murcott, Gower Publishing, 1983, pp.18–30.

Unti, Bernard. '"Peace on Earth Among the Orders of Creation": Vegetarian Ethics in the Unites States Before World War 1.' *Routledge History of Food*, edited by Carol Helstosky, Routledge, 2014, pp. 179–99. *ProQuest Ebook Central*, ebookcentral.proquest.com/lib/unimelb/detail.action?docID=1811096.

West, Michael. *Vampires Don't Sparkle! Anthology*. Seventh Star Press, 2013.

Wester, Maisha, and Xavier Aldana Reyes. *Twenty-First-Century Gothic: An Edinburgh Companion*. Edinburgh UP, 2019.

'What is a Vegetarian?' Vegetarian Society, Oct. 2016, www.vegsoc.org/definition. Accessed 15 July 2018.

Williamson, Milly. *The Lure of the Vampire: Gender, Fiction and Fandom from Bram Stoker to Buffy*. Wallflower Press, 2005.

Wolfe, Cary. *Animal Rites: American Culture, the Discourse of Species, and Posthumanist Theory*. Chicago UP, 2003.

Wright, Laura. *The Vegan Studies Project: Food, Animals, and Gender in the Age of Terror*. Georgia UP, 2015. *JSTOR*, www.jstor.org/stable/j.ctt183q3vb.

Zalasiewicz, Jan, et al. 'The New World of the Anthropocene.' *Environmental Science and Technology*, vol. 44, no. 7, Apr. 2010, pp. 2228–31. *EBSCOhost*, https://doi.org/10.1021/es903118j.

Film and TV

Being Human. Created by Toby Whithouse, BBC Three, 2009–13.

Being Human. Created by Toby Whithouse, developed by Jeremy Carver and Anna Fricke, Syfy, 2011–14.

Black as Night. Directed by Maritte Lee Go, Amazon Studios, 2021.

Blade. Directed by Stephen Norrington, New Line Cinema, 1998.

Blade: Trinity. Directed by David S. Goyer, New Line Cinema, 2004.

Blade II. Directed by Guillermo del Toro, New Line Cinema, 2002.

'Bloodlust.' Directed by Robert Singer. *Supernatural*, season 2, episode 3, The CW, 12 Oct. 2006. Amazon *Prime Video*, https://www.primevideo.com/.

Chapelwaite. Created by Jason Filardi and Peter Filardi, Epix, 2021.

Daybreakers. Directed by Michael Spierig and Peter Spierig, Lionsgate, 2009.

Discovery of Witches. Created by Deborah Harkness. Sky Vision / NBCUniversal, 2018–22.

Dracula. Created by Mark Gatiss and Steven Moffat, Netflix, 2020.

Dracula. Created by Cole Haddon and Daniel Knauff, NBC / Sky Living, 2013.

Firebite. Created by Warwick Thornton and Brendan Fletcher, AMC, 2021–.

Fright Night. Directed by Craig Gillespie, Walt Disney Studios Motion Pictures, 2011.

A Girl Walks Home Alone at Night. Directed by Ana Lily Amirpour, Vice Films / Kino Lorber, 2014.

I Am Legend. Directed by Francis Lawrence, Warner Bros. Pictures, 2007.

Legacies. Created by Julie Plec, The CW, 2018–22.

Let the Right One In. Directed by Tomas Alfredson, Sandrew Metronome, 2008.

Midnight Mass. Created by Mike Flanagan, Netflix, 2021.

The Mortal Instruments: City of Bones. Directed by Harald Zwart, Sony Pictures Releasing, 2013.

NOS4A2. Created by Jami O'Brien, AMC, 2019.

Only Lovers Left Alive. Directed by Jim Jarmusch, Soda Pictures, 2013.

The Passage. Created by Liz Heldins, Fox, 2019.

Pride, Prejudice and Zombies. Directed by Burr Stevens, Lionsgate / Sony Pictures Releasing, 2016.

Priest. Directed by Scott Stewart, Sony Pictures Releasing, 2011.

Shadowhunters. Developed by Ed Decter, The CW, 2016–19.

Stakeland. Directed by Jim Mickle, Dark Sky Films / IFC Films, 2010.

Stoker, Bram. Dracula. Rev. ed., Penguin Group, 2003.

The Strain. Created by Guillermo del Toro and Chuck Hogan, FX, 2014–17.

Thirst. Directed by Park Chan-woo, Focus Features LLC, 2009.

30 Days of Nights. Directed by David Slade, Sony Pictures Releasing, 2007.

Ultraviolet. Created by Joe Ahearne, Channel 4, 1998.

Underworld. Directed by Len Wiseman, Screen Gems, 2003.

Underworld: Awakening. Directed by Måns Mårlind and Björn Stein, Sony Pictures Releasing, 2012.

Underworld: Blood Wars. Directed by Anna Foerster, Sony Pictures Releasing, 2016.

Underworld: Evolution. Directed by Len Wiseman, Sony Pictures Releasing, 2006.

Underworld: Rise of the Lycans. Directed by Patrick Tatopoulous, Sony Pictures Releasing, 2009.

V Wars. Created by William Laurin and Glenn Davis, Netflix, 2019.

CHAPTER 2

Rat's Blood and Rice: Interview with the Proto-vegetarian Vampire

Abstract This chapter takes Anne Rice's depiction of Louis de Pointe du Lac's reluctant vampirism in *Interview with the Vampire* as the starting point for later articulations of vegetarian vampirism. More specifically, it argues that Louis is the proto-vegetarian vampire, the prototype or preliminary version from which later forms are developed. The chapter first places Louis's animal-blood diet in a longer tradition of vampire fiction and film (*House of Dracula*, *Dark Shadows*), which features vampires who attempt to stop drinking human blood. The chapter then provides a summary of the key elements of the proto-vegetarian vampire and the type of life this opens up. These elements remain embryonic in *Interview* as a result of the novel's chief concern, namely, the morality of the sympathetic vampire, analysed in the next part of the chapter. The chapter concludes with the acknowledgement that while its vampiric inheritors in *Buffy*, *Twilight* and *The Vampire Diaries*, but not *The Southern Vampire Mysteries* or *True Blood*, largely evolve past *Interview*'s sympathetic initiative to consider vampiric vegetarianism as an ethical enterprise, they are nevertheless indebted to Rice's proto-vegetarian vampire.

Keywords Anne Rice • Animal-blood diet • Sympathetic vampire • Louis de Pointe du Lac • *Interview with the Vampire*

S. Dungan, *Reading the Vegetarian Vampire*, Palgrave Gothic, https://doi.org/10.1007/978-3-031-18350-8_2

In the first decade of the twenty-first century, we find in our books and on our screens—with increasing regularity—vampires who choose to drink animal or synthetic but not human blood. Although most contemporary vampires still drink human blood (a defining feature of the traditional vampire), those who have made the change are the most popular and prominent. Despite being the minority amongst their species, there has nevertheless been a rather conspicuous surge in texts that choose to incorporate at least one vegetarian vampire. However, before vegetarian vampires became commonplace, before there was Edward Cullen, Stefan Salvatore or Bill Compton, there was Louis de Pointe du Lac, the reluctant vampire at the heart of Anne Rice's *Interview with the Vampire* (1976), who subsists (temporarily, at least) on a diet of animal blood, drawn from rats and dogs.

Critics have discussed Louis's animal-blood diet with attention to questions of gender (Keller 16; Tomc), melodrama (Williamson, *Lure* 41–43), agency (Davidel), and post-existentialism (Waxman 89). Still others treat his diet as an analogy for addiction (Fahy 122–27) and disordered eating (Ní Fhlainn 33–34) or argue Louis's diet and his beauty reflect 'the aspirational goal of 1980s exercise and weight-loss culture' (Fahy 12; Ní Fhlainn 48). Few mention exactly how unusual and radical Louis's animal-blood diet was in the late-twentieth century. This may be because Louis subsists on animal blood for only a brief period (70 pages in a novel of 308 pages),[1] after which he turns to a diet of human blood. Further, this interlude is peripheral to the novel as a whole, which records Louis's life history and 'spans several hundred years … of a Faustian search for some meaning to his life-in-death existence' (Parker 1144). This oversight may also be owing to the novel's radical overhaul of vampire fiction as a whole, in which Louis's short-lived diet of animal blood is merely one of many revisions of the genre. As Candace Benefiel observes, in the years before *Interview* was published, the literary and cinematic vampire was:

> stuck in the mold into which he had been cast by Bram Stoker … —an essentially solitary predator whose presence was the stimulus for an intrepid group of vampire hunters to form and bay in his pursuit, and whose time on centre stage was limited to brief, menacing appearances and capped with a spectacular death scene. The vampire was, to borrow a term from film, a

---

[1] This period amounts to the first 'four years' (70) of Louis's vampire life.

McGuffin—a device to drive the plot and give the vampire hunters something to pursue. (261)

With *Interview*, Rice 'turned [Stoker's] paradigm on its head' (Benefiel
261). Not only do her vampires (with the exception of Claudia and
Madeline) not die, they are the protagonists and antagonists of their own
story; a story that comes from the vampire himself. This is the first time
'we hear the "other" speaking firsthand' (Gelder 109) and 'the result is
that the vampires, rather than signifying a fear of the dangerous and taboo,
are presented as sympathetic and knowable "outsiders"' (Williamson, *Lure*
40). Other significant revisions to the genre include the vampire's shift
from solitary to communal modes of existence (Zanger 18),[2] from the
magical to the mundane (vampires' folkloric powers are 'bullshit'
[*Interview* 22]) and from incarnations of absolute evil to creatures who
have the potential to do good (Zanger 18–19).[3] Further, they are now
creatures able to reflect on their own lives, with a penchant for philosophical inquiry (Waxman 79), who want to become aware of their own history
and origins (Auerbach 152); and who, when they explore the world, find
'an entire subculture based on their own peculiar existence' (Benefiel 262).

Rather than focusing on these shifts, which have been discussed at
length, in this chapter I foreground the period in which Louis subsisted
on animal blood. Although short-lived, its significance becomes obvious
when we place this episode in dialogue with the later vampire fictions considered in this book.[4] After all, it is Louis who chooses, for the first time in
vampire fiction, to subsist on a diet of animal blood. By introducing this
narrative twist, the novel establishes animal blood as a viable dietary alternative to human blood. It is possible, then, to argue that Louis's non-
standard animal-blood diet is an anticipation of and an influence on later

[2] Many critics read Lestat, Louis and Claudia as composing a queer nuclear family. See, for
example, Haggerty, and for a particularly insightful analysis of this trend, see Gelder, Chapter
Six. For a contrasting view, see Keller 8–19.
[3] For a discussion of other revisions that *Interview* makes to the genre, see Benefiel; Wood;
Zanger; and Zimmermann.
[4] Here my argument differs from Laura Wright's, who reads Louis's diet as participating in
the historical tradition of *Dracula* where 'such consumption has signified both weakness and
empathy'. She remarks that 'in *Dracula,* Renfield, although he is not a "real" vampire, is
forced to feed on small creatures—spiders, flies and rats—because he has no access to larger
creatures or humans, while in *Interview* Lestat chastises Louis, calling him a "whining cow-
ard of a vampire who prowls the night killing alley cats and rats"' (48).

vampire fictions. In other words, Louis is the proto-vegetarian vampire,[5] the prototype or preliminary version from which later forms are developed. As the term preliminary suggests, although some of the key elements of the vegetarian vampire are present, they are not yet fully developed. Nonetheless, as this chapter will argue, in *Interview* we can see the first signs of what will later become the vegetarian vampire, and it is these signs, and their influence on later iterations of the vegetarian vampire, that this chapter sets out to explore.

Refusing to Feed: The Twentieth-Century Tradition

To illustrate exactly how unusual, in the context of vampire fiction, Louis's animal-blood diet was, it is necessary to sketch some of the features of the genre to which it belongs. When *Interview* was published, there was an already long, although niche, tradition of vampires who tried to stop drinking human blood. This tradition extends as far back as 1945, to Universal Pictures' *House of Dracula*, in which Dracula and the Wolf Man (the supernatural beings at the centre of this film), having grown tired of their afflictions, attempt to find ways of escaping the respective curses under which they labour (Williamson, *Lure* 43). This storyline is also featured in the popular daytime soap-opera *Dark Shadows* (1966–71). Like the Dracula of *House of Dracula* before him, Barnabas Collins, the show's vampiric protagonist, seeks to cure his thirst for human blood and asks Dr. Julia Hoffman to perform experiments on him to that end. What is interesting is that Barnabas had not always been tormented by his thirst. In early episodes, he was simply a McGuffin, 'originally intended to be a traditional evil vampire who would be staked after a few months of thrills and peril for the human characters'. Indeed, the early Barnabas 'was always on the verge of violence' (Day 38). However, he proved too popular with the audience to be confined to a handful of menacing appearances—the series' ratings doubled after he became part of the story (Lampley 85)—so the writers went back to 1795 to tell the story of how Barnabas became a vampire under the spell of the witch Angelique. What the audience saw was a 'thoroughly decent and likable' human Barnabas who, when he becomes a vampire, 'struggles with his urges, though he cannot conquer

---

[5] I borrow this term from Adam Shprintzen, who uses proto-vegetarianism to refer to 'the individuals and groups who lay the foundations of a vegetarian movement in the United States' (10).

them' (Day 38). From then on, he plays the part of 'a reluctant vampire doomed to eternal life and a fruitless search for a cure for his affliction' (Lampley 85).[6]

As *Dark Shadows* attests, already by 1970 it was possible to imagine a vampire whose hunger, no longer a singular drive, was a source of internal conflict; and therefore, also to imagine a vampire with a psychological and moral complexity not seen in earlier incarnations of the vampire. As Day points out, '*Dark Shadows* became the story of a vampire turning into an image of humanity as Barnabas changed ... from a deadly menace to the saviour of the Collins family ... [He] aspired to what the audience wanted—to be free, to be loved, to be part of a family' (39). Yet, try as Barnabas might to be free of his thirst for human blood, his hopes are never realised. Despite his desire to be otherwise than he is, Barnabas remains a slave to his need and desire for human blood.

THE PROTO-VEGETARIAN VAMPIRE

At this intersection between free will and biological drive, we can start to locate Rice's revision of vampire mythology and diet. In contrast to the story of Dracula in the *House of Dracula* and of Barnabas in *Dark Shadows*, rather than seeking to extinguish her vampire's bloodlust, Rice offers a radical alternative. By allowing the vampire's biological need for blood to be satiated by animal blood, she offers a novel solution to Barnabas's struggle, one that bifurcates the vampires' previously singular dietary path. Although Louis does succumb before long to his natural craving for human blood, the key point is that he *can* and *does* (for a time) choose to consume animal rather than human blood. In other words, Louis ushers in the vampire's capacity to *choose* not to drink from humans, to drink instead from animals. Lestat chooses to remain as he has always been: 'animals gave [Lestat] no satisfaction whatsoever. [They] were to be banked on when all else failed, but never to be chosen' (74). But Louis chooses to veer from his 'true nature' and embrace the kind of life opened up to him by animal blood.

That life includes the ability to be good. As Jules Zanger observes, as a result of Louis's choice, 'the vampire's absolutely evil nature as [seen] in *Dracula* becomes increasingly compromised, permitting the existence of

---

[6] For a discussion of the importance of *Dark Shadows* to the canon, see Day 35–43; Lampley 84–89; Skal 70; Spooner; Williamson, 'Television'; and Zimmermann 104.

"good" vampires as well as bad ones' (18–19). David Punter makes a similar point when he writes that 'Louis is a *good* vampire; not very good, to be sure, since he kills nightly, but he does make an attempt to kill only animals, like a kind of vegetarian bloodsucker' (161). Insofar as it complicates the vampire's traditional role as an 'evil' villain, then, this choice signals more than a decision to forgo one's natural food source: it signals the vampire's capacity for moral judgement, which in turn introduces (even if only in embryo) the possibility of less destructive interactions with (and integration into) human society.

That animal blood introduces 'the good' into the evil world of the vampire is owing to the morality that guides Louis to choose to consume animal blood. First, his choice to live on a diet of rats and dogs is a choice to not harm humans. As he tells Lestat, 'if I can live from the blood of animals, why should I not live from the blood of animals rather than go through the world bringing misery and death to human creatures!' (77). In that regard, animal blood serves as the single greatest expression of Louis's sympathy and care for humans. This finds particular emphasis if we compare his decision not to feed on humans to the choices made by Lestat and Claudia, whose 'delight in blood-drinking and [the] wanton destruction of human life [is] emblematic of [their] villainy' (Williamson, *Lure* 42). Whereas Louis is motivated by a desire to spare (and not cause) human suffering, Lestat is motivated by a desire to maximise human suffering. This desire is registered in his choice of victims: 'a fresh young girl' or a 'young man', for they represent 'the greatest loss', situated as they are 'on the threshold of the maximum possibility of life' (41). As for Claudia, as she freely admits, she has 'no human nature' (108): 'I kill humans every night. I seduce them, draw them close to me, with an insatiable hunger, a constant never-ending search for something … and I care nothing about them—where they came from, where they would go' (114). All she cares for, she says, is a communion with 'my own kind' (136).

Second, drinking animal blood is also an empathetic act. As Lestat tells Louis, 'you wander through the night, feeding on rats like a pauper … filled with care' (77). Lestat's suggestion that a diet of animal blood not only allows one to care for humans but is informed by a sense of care for humans is perhaps one of the most important aspects of Louis's alternate diet, opening the possibility that the gap between humans and vampires could be bridged. Louis's affection for Babette is a prime example of this. As the boy observes, 'the way you speak of [Babette], [it is] as if your feeling was special' (56). He is shocked to find out, in turn, that what Louis feels is love. Louis admits, 'I feel love, and I felt some measure of love for Babette' (57). Here we have the first suggestion that vampires and humans could establish close relations with each other if the vampire was able to change his diet. Although this is only a suggestion (Babette does not reciprocate Louis's affection—she tries to kill him once he reveals his true nature to her [66]), Louis's love for Babette shows that a vegetarian diet allows him, if only briefly, to step out of predator-prey relations with humans.

Unsurprisingly, the ability to love and care for humans does not extend to vampires who consume human blood. This is already implicit in the delight taken by Lestat in human suffering and in Claudia's fascination with poverty and, further, in their shared penchant for decimating entire families (Claudia even picks off her own family 'one by one' [96]). It is confirmed once Louis turns to a diet of human blood and acknowledges that, with his new diet and 'life of nightly killing, I had grown far from the attachment I'd felt for [Babette] ... my sister or any mortal' (120). No longer able to view humans 'with the great love [he had] felt for [his] sister and Babette', Louis just sees 'pulsing victims ... with some new detachment and need' (91). With this distinction, *Interview* makes explicit the power of the animal blood diet to engender human-vampire (inter-species) relationships that are quite different to those engendered by a diet of human blood. If the latter keeps the predator-prey relationship intact, it makes sense that a diet of animal blood allows that relationship to be negotiated or loosened as the vampire seeks a different prey. The vampire can consequently seek out and discover other needs that are not singularly tied to hunger. Together, then, the possibilities of love between creatures from different species and even the responsibility of one species for another, which are anticipated but not fully realised by Louis, work as a precursor to the types of relations between vampires and humans that appear in later fictions, especially the radically romantic (for the time being), reciprocal and nonconsumptive relationship between Buffy and Angel, and Buffy and Spike in *Buffy*.

It is worth adding that, in *Interview*, Louis is not the only vampire to feed on animal blood. In *Interview*'s mythology, the consumption of animal blood is a necessity 'from time to time' (33). Lestat makes this revelation to Louis as part of a lesson on the mechanics of vampiric travel, advising that sometimes, in order to pass unseen by human eyes, one must feed on animals. Particularly if 'travelling by ship', Lestat remarks, 'you damn well better live off rats, if you don't wish to cause such a panic on board that they search your coffin' (33). This is important for two reasons: it introduces strict parameters for acceptable animal-blood consumption and it tags animal blood as a viable (even if not tasty) dietary option for all vampires, not just those who want to travel safely. This development situates Louis's non-standard diet within a set of food behaviours wider than those usually found in earlier vampire fiction. What makes Louis's decision to subsist on animal blood so radical and influential, then, is not that he drinks animal blood but that he makes it (and Rice introduces it as) a lifestyle. In so doing he turns the exception into the quotidian: Louis takes what Lestat calls *occasionally* necessary and makes it the new normal, at least for him, for a time.

'A VILE UNSUPPORTABLE HUNGER': LOUIS'S HUMAN-BLOOD DIET

Although Rice brings new blood to vampire fiction, she does not fully develop a dietary ethic in relation to which Louis's proto-vegetarianism can be placed. David Punter suggests as much when he writes, 'there is a sense in which Rice shirks the questions which lie behind Louis's condition' (161). The moral ambiguity behind Louis's diet is apparent if we look at the broader inter-species interactions informed by it, or rather the lack thereof. In comparison to later fictions such as *Twilight*, *The Vampire Diaries*, *The Southern Vampire Mysteries* and *True Blood*, where a diet of animal (or synthetic) blood forms the basis of a multispecies world in which humans and vampires live amongst one another, cohabitating and comingling in a good example of cross-species interchange, Louis never integrates with the human world. Unlike the Cullens, Angel, Spike or Bill, he does not try to help humans (apart from Babette); all he does is watch (Auerbach 154). He watches at Babette's window as 'helpless as the goddess who came by night to watch Endymion sleep and could not have him' (77), just as he watches Claudia kill, even though the experience is 'chilling' (93). *Interview*'s world, thus, is not one of cross-species cohabitation and community, as we come to find in later texts, but insular, one of 'ornamental self-enclosure' (Auerbach 155).[7]

---

[7] Though not contemplated in *Interview*, Rice does develop a cross-species ethic in *The Vampire Lestat* (1985). For a discussion of this development, see Gordon, 'Rehabilitating Revenants' and Waxman 93–95.

This self-enclosure is owing to Rice's construction of vampires as 'multiple, communal, and familial, living with and relating to other vampires' (Zanger 18). Prior to *Interview*, the vampire was a solitary figure—and the text revisits (and keeps intact) that figure in the form of the zombified vampires that Louis and Claudia encounter in Transylvania. However, as we see with *Interview*'s central vampiric groupings—the family that Louis, Lestat, and Claudia form and the Theatres des Vampires—'almost all essential relationships are between vampire and vampire' (Zanger 21). (The exceptions to this would be Louis and Babette, Claudia and Madeleine—who does, admittedly, become a vampire—and Lestat and his human boy).[8] *Interview* is simply not interested in human affairs. Its vampires are, as Nina Auerbach writes, 'self-absorbed' with 'cosmic longings' that concern only 'the discovery of [their] own origin, not the salvation of mortals' (152). Indeed, much of the narrative is devoted to Louis's efforts to discover and understand 'what is it that is our nature' (77), and the lingering questions that drive Louis's time in Europe are why vampires exist, why vampires were created or 'allowed to begin' and 'how under god [they] might be ended' (153). Unsurprisingly, this shift to a vampire-centric narrative leaves humans to their natural (in the scheme of vampire fiction) role of food (Zanger 21), 'the rich feasts that conscience cannot appreciate' (82).

Thus, the chief concerns that drive *Interview*'s vampires are very different from those that influence later vampires like Spike, Edward and Bill, who in the context of their own fictions love, help and want to live amongst humans. The animal-blood diet enables the authors of these later fictions to draw the contours of (and so imagine) a multispecies world in which different species, as represented by humans and vampires, are not bound to a set of hierarchical relations in which humans are at the centre and the animal-other is on the margins, and this enables less destructive cross-species relationships to emerge. In *Interview*, this possibility is present only in the embryo. As much as Louis's attempt at vegetarianism is presented as a means to mitigate human suffering, *Interview*, with its

[8] The extent to which Lestat fits into this category is questionable because, as he tells Louis, his relationship with the boy is not one of love; instead, he says, 'it excites me to be close to him, to think over and over, I can kill him and I will kill him but not now. And then to leave him and find someone who looks nearly like him as possible. If he had brothers... why I'd kill them one by one. The family would succumb to a mysterious fever which dried up the very blood in their bodies!' (119).

vampire-centric focus, ultimately maintains (perhaps even strengthens) the lines between species.[9]

What we find in *Interview* instead, and what is developed through Louis's choice to consume animal blood, is the morality of the sympathetic vampire. (Indeed, Rice is, as Gerhards observes, 'often cited as the mother of the sympathetic vampire type and the flourishing subgenre around it' [240].) Best understood as 'a creature troubled by its ontology', the sympathetic vampire 'is a being at odds with its vampiric body and the urges that this body generates' (Williamson, 'Television' par. 2). As noted earlier, the vampire's chief urge is blood hunger, and Louis's struggle with his vampiric appetite is well documented throughout the novel. We are told, for example, that he has too much human nature to embrace his vampiric nature and feed on human blood; and Louis himself laments over his thirst for human blood, which he describes as 'a vile unsupportable hunger' (106). Louis's conflict with his vampire nature is again revealed as he questions Lestat as to why he is 'such a vampire as you are! Vengeful and delighting in taking human life, even when you have no need', and again as he questions Lestat, who feeds on and kills two prostitutes 'when one would have done' (75–76). Lestat provides Louis with a simple answer: 'what lies before you is vampire nature, which is killing'. But Louis rejects such an answer, claiming 'that's how *you* see it!' (77).

Louis's struggle comes down to his belief that his thirst for human blood makes him 'damned' (68)—a view which indicates a degree of self-awareness and capacity for self-judgement that are defining features of the sympathetic vampire that Rice is pioneering in this novel. As he tells Armand toward *Interview*'s end, 'I'm evil, evil as any vampire who ever lived! I've killed over and over and will do it again' (213). Here we discern the sympathetic work that diet does in *Interview*. Like Barnabas before him, Louis struggles with his thirst for human blood and attempts to feed differently. Again characteristic of the sympathetic vampire that Rice constructs, Louis attempts to cure his hunger and reject the typical lifestyle of his species as represented by Lestat and Claudia, 'which is killing' (77). Louis reveals to Armand that he 'wanted love and goodness in this which is living death' (303) and his diet of animal blood was his way of achieving that. However, this attempt is in vain; a diet of animal blood only adds to

[9] Deborah Mutch writes that the separation between species is 'maintained' throughout the novel by 'the mechanical interface of the tape recorder' (7).

Louis's existential pain and brings him nothing but 'discontent' (81), alienating him from his vampiric peers.

Louis turns to human blood, desperate to experience Lestat's 'guarantee' that a proper vampiric diet will erase Louis's anguish and any 'hunger left [for] Babette' (77) and any nostalgia for his human life. As it transpires, Lestat's promise holds true—when Louis kills humans 'there is no longing' (82). But this realisation only increases his suffering. As he tells the boy, 'my agony was unbearable. Never since I was a human being had I felt such mental pain. It was because Lestat's words had made sense to me. I knew peace only when I killed, only for that minute' (81). Here we recognize the existential struggle of the sympathetic vampire. Even when Louis submits to his hunger and is free of the turmoil that comes with a diet of animal blood, he cannot be free of the guilt that comes as the price of knowing that killing and drinking another's blood is wrong.

Louis's struggle with his need for human blood continues to *Interview*'s end. Although he submits to a rather regular, nightly diet of human blood, he never resorts to the sadistic feeding practices that Claudia and Lestat engage in. Instead, and in keeping with his sympathetic nature, Louis lets the hunger 'accumulate ... in me, till the drive grew almost too strong, so that I might give myself to it all the more completely, blindly' (103–04). As Barbara Waxman points out, Louis 'knows that he is constrained by his compulsion to kill' (88), but by waiting he sidesteps the moral conundrum that feeding on human blood presents him with. By hunting this way, Louis attempts to absolve his own guilt as he tells himself that it is his biological need to 'kill ... which is pulling me' and making him kill, 'I am not pulling the string. The string is pulling me' (115). While such a method of feeding—one which causes Lestat to label Louis 'Merciful Death' (96)—is still predatory—no matter how Louis tries to reconcile this truth within himself otherwise—there is something to be said for how Louis feeds, namely, that it is inextricably tied to his sentience. Like Claudia and Lestat, Louis is self-aware; but unlike his companions, he feels guilt. As Joan Gordon writes

> [Louis'] sentience makes him aware of the suffering of his prey, and [their] existence not just as a species but as an individual. Such awareness ... makes predation and survival a moral conundrum. When [Louis] sees his prey as individuals, cares for and loves a few of those individuals, he can no longer function as a predator ... The thinking predator cannot resolve his survival

with the killing it necessitates; so, he must sacrifice his awareness. ('Rehabilitating Revenants' 232)

This kind of sentience, new to vampire fiction and to the vampires around him, opens up the path for later vampire fictions to imagine vampires who are no longer constrained by their nature and their need to feed on human blood. Vampires like Edward, Stefan and Bill are attuned to human suffering and do what Louis is unable to do: abstain from human blood. Louis's sentience and his revised feeding habits are nevertheless the first steps towards this later development. Indeed, it would appear that abandoning a diet of human blood altogether is the natural, if not necessary, next step for a predator whose very sentience 'makes predation and survival a moral conundrum' (Gordon, 'Rehabilitating Revenants' 232).

Despite his efforts to be a different kind of vampire by killing humans swiftly and taking only what he needs, Louis arrives at the conclusion that there is no redemption for a vampire. This includes his attempt to be and do good by feeding on animal blood. As he tells Armand,

> What I asked was impossible … from the beginning, because you cannot have love and goodness when you do what you know to be evil, what you know to be wrong … I knew it when I first took a human life to feed my craving … and it was all the same, all evil. And all wrong. (303)

Although Armand attempts to assuage Louis's despair, pointing out that there are 'gradations of evil' and that evil is not 'a great perilous gulf into which one falls with the first sin, plummeting to the depth' (213), Louis refuses to be told otherwise. As he tells the boy, 'no one could in any guise convince me of what I myself knew to be true, that I was damned in my own mind and soul' (303).

In summary, we can say that diet is used in *Interview* to create a degree of sympathy for the vampire that would be unthinkable in previous vampire texts. As Waxman observes, 'Louis emerges as an appealing, remorseful, though obsessive, killer: [and] his obsessive need to kill makes him a victim of his nature' (92). This enables Rice to make another contribution to the possibilities explored by future vampire fictions. By having Louis struggle so desperately with his thirst, he emerges, to rephrase Punter, as 'a *good* vampire; [although] not very good' (161). As Armand points out, there are 'gradations of evil' (213) and *Interview* reveals these gradations as being grounded in diet. What separates Louis out from the rest (not in his mind, but in ours) is his attempt to kill only animals and to do (or feed) better than his counterparts. With Louis, *Interview* therefore opens up the essentialist depiction of vampires and vampiric diets and, in so doing, enables readers to disagree fundamentally with Louis's assertion that he is simply evil. What *Interview* shows us instead is that vampires who drink human blood are not necessarily or completely evil. Though he still feeds on human blood, there is a developed sensibility or humanity, and a deliberate step away from predatory ethics, not seen in previous incarnations of the vampire. By depicting the vampire's blood hunger in more sympathetic terms, Rice takes the first step towards making it possible to imagine a vampire who not only refuses to consume human blood but is able both to adhere to that decision and turn it into a lifestyle. Still more importantly, in Louis's awareness of the pain felt by humans and his sense of guilt, we find the embryonic ethics of the vegetarian vampire. Although its vampiric inheritors in *Buffy*, *Twilight* and *The Vampire Diaries*, but not *The Southern Vampire Mysteries* or *True Blood* (as I shall discuss later), largely evolve past *Interview*'s sympathetic initiative to consider vampiric vegetarianism as an ethical enterprise, they are nevertheless indebted to Rice's proto-vegetarian vampire. Louis may claim that he is 'not the spirit of any age' (258), but as the following chapters will show, he looks forward to the spirit of our vampire age.

WORKS CITED

Benefiel, Candace R. 'Blood Relations: The Gothic Perversion of the Nuclear Family in Anne Rice's *Interview with the Vampire*.' *Journal of Popular Culture*, vol. 38, no. 2, 2004, pp. 261–73. *Wiley Online Library*, https://doi.org/10.1111/j.0022-3840.2004.00111.x.

Davidel, Laura. 'Agency in the Ricean Vampire's Compulsion to Feed.' *Mearcstapa: Ten Years of Teratology*, special issue of *Preternature: Critical and Historical Studies on the Preternatural*, vol. 9, no. 1, 2020, pp. 97–121. *Project MUSE*, muse.jhu.edu/article/748832.

Day, William Patrick. *Vampire Legends in Contemporary American Culture: What Becomes a Legend Most*. Kentucky UP, 2015. *ProQuest Ebook Central*, ebookcentral.proquest.com/lib/unimelb/detail.action?docID=1915342.

Fahy, Thomas. *Dining with Madmen: Fat, Food, and the Environment in 1980s Horror*. Mississippi UP, 2019.

Gelder, Ken. *Reading the Vampire*. Routledge, 1994.

Gordon, Joan. 'Rehabilitating Revenants, or Sympathetic Vampires in Recent Fiction.' *Extrapolation*, vol. 29, no. 3, 1988, pp. 227–34.

Gordon, Joan, and Veronica Hollinger, editors. *Blood Read: The Vampire as Metaphor in Contemporary Culture.* Pennsylvania UP, 1997.

Haggerty, George E. 'Anne Rice and the Queering of Culture.' *Reading Gender After Feminism,* special issue of *NOVEL: A Forum on* Fiction, vol. 32, no. 1, autumn 1998, pp. 5–18. *JSTOR,* www.jstor.org/stable/1346054.

Keller, James. *Anne Rice and Sexual Politics: The Early Novels.* McFarland, 2000.

Lampley, Jonathan Malcolm. 'Dark Shadows.' *The Essential Cult TV Reader,* edited by David Lavery, Kentucky UP, 2010, pp. 84–89. *JSTOR,* www.jstor.org/stable/j.ctt130jj8f.

Mutch, Deborah. *The Modern Vampire and Human Identity.* Palgrave Macmillan, 2013.

Nayar, Pramod K. *Posthumanism.* Polity, 2014.

Ní Fhlainn, Sorcha. *Postmodern Vampires: Film, Fiction, and Popular Culture.* Palgrave Macmillan, 2019. *Springer Link,* https://doi.org/10.1057/978-1-137-58377-2.

Parker, Julia. Review of *Interview with the Vampire,* by Anne Rice. *Library Journal,* vol. 101, no. 9, 1 May 1976, p. 1144. *EBSCOhost,* discovery.ebsco.com/link-processor/plink?id=db4f333b-910b-3f81-8f80-af5cbbf200c8.

Punter, David. *The Literature of Terror: A History of Gothic Fictions from 1975 to the Present Day.* Vol 2, Addison Wesley Longman Ltd, 1996.

Rice, Anne. *Interview with the Vampire.* 1976. Sphere, 2008.

Shprintzen, Adam D. *The Vegetarian Crusade: The Rise of an American Reform Movement, 1817–1921.* North Carolina UP, 2013. *JSTOR,* https://doi.org/10.5149/9781469608921_shprintzen.

Skal, David. *V Is for Vampire: The A-Z Guide to Everything Undead.* Plume, 1996.

Spooner, Catherine. '"Last Night I Dreamt I Went to Collinwood Again": Vampire Adaptation and Reincarnation Romance in *Dark Shadows.*' *Horror Studies,* vol. 8, no. 2, Oct. 2017, pp. 205–22. *Ingenta Connect,* https://doi.org/10.1386/host.8.2.205_1.

Tomc, Sandra. 'Dieting and Damnation: Anne Rice's *Interview with the Vampire.*' Gordon and Hollinger, pp. 95–113.

The Vampire Lestat. Little, Brown, 1985.

Waxman, Barbara Frey. 'Postexistentialism in the Neo-Gothic Mode: Anne Rice's *Interview with the Vampire.*' *Mosaic: An Interdisciplinary Critical Journal,* vol. 25, no. 3, summer 1992, pp. 79–97. *JSTOR,* www.jstor.org/stable/24780429.

Williamson, Milly. *The Lure of the Vampire: Gender, Fiction and Fandom from Bram Stoker to Buffy.* Wallflower Press, 2005.

———. 'Television, Vampires and the Body: Somatic Pathos.' *Mysterious Bodies,* special issue of *Intensities: Journal of Cult Media,* edited by Rayna Denison and Mark Jancovich, vol. 4, autumn/winter, 2007, intensitiescultmedia.files.wordpress.com/2012/12/williamson-television-vampires-and-the-body.pdf.

Wood, Martin J. 'New Life for an Old Tradition: Anne Rice and Vampire Literature.' *The Blood Is the Life: Vampires in Literature*, edited by Leonard G. Heldreth and Mary Pharr, Bowling Green State UP, 1999, pp. 59–78.

Wright, Laura. *The Vegan Studies Project: Food, Animals, and Gender in the Age of Terror*. Georgia UP, 2015. *JSTOR*, www.jstor.org/stable/j.ctt183q3vb.

Zanger, Jules. 'Metaphor into Metonymy: The Vampire Next Door.' Gordon and Hollinger, pp. 17–26.

Zimmermann, Gail Abbott. 'The World of the Vampire: Rice's Contribution.' *The Anne Rice Reader: Writers Explore the Universes of Anne Rice*, edited by Katherine Ramsand, Ballantine books, 1997, pp. 101–23.

FILM AND TV

Dark Shadows. Created by Dan Curtis, ABC, 1966–71.

House of Dracula. Directed by Erle E. Kenton, Universal Pictures, 1945.

CHAPTER 3

Pig's Blood and the Politics of Choice in *Buffy the Vampire Slayer*

Abstract This chapter examines the television series *Buffy the Vampire Slayer*, in order to trace the next stage in the emergence of the vegetarian vampire. This series features not one but two human-blood-abstinent vampires (Angel and Spike), along with some key developments, made possible by an animal-blood diet, that anticipate the inter-species relationships later seen in *Mysteries* and *True Blood*. These developments remain embryonic in *Buffy* as a result of the series' treatment of 'vegetarian' modes of feeding as well as the constraints of the slayer narrative. Nonetheless, a diet of animal-blood leads Angel and Spike to a series of important changes in character including the ability to care for and love humans, analysed in the next part of the chapter. The last section considers the constraints of the slayer narrative, which shapes the show as a whole and so conditions its depiction of human-vampire relations.

Keywords Animal-blood diet • *Buffy the Vampire Slayer* •
Angel • Spike

In the cult television series *Buffy the Vampire Slayer* (1997–2003), we encounter, in Angel and Spike, two more late-twentieth-century iterations of the human-blood-abstinent vampire. Like Louis before them, Angel and Spike both refrain, for an extended period of time, from drinking human blood. However, unlike Louis, Angel and Spike do not ever make a conscious choice to drink animal rather than human blood; indeed, they are never in a position where they are free to make this choice. Further, in the series as a whole, very little is made of the period during which Angel and Spike abstain from human blood. Across *Buffy*'s seven seasons and the spin-off series *Angel*, which ran for five seasons, Angel's and Spike's animal-blood diet is mentioned only twice. In *Angel*, Angel remarks on one occasion that the pig's blood he is drinking tastes better than usual (he is unaware that it has been spiked with human blood) (Wright 48). In *Buffy*, Spike's consumption of pig's blood in the season four episode 'Something Blue' prompts Giles 'to refer to him as an "impotent" "help-less creature"' (Wright 48–49).

Perhaps as a result of *Buffy*'s sporadic engagement with matters of diet,[1] few critics have discussed in detail Angel's and Spike's human-blood absti-nence despite the plethora of edited collections and commentaries that discuss *Buffy* from a variety of perspectives.[2] While many have discussed Angel's and Spike's souls (Erickson; Kind; Magnusson; McLaren), hybrid-ity (Abbott, *Undead Apocalypse* 120–24; Bailey; Hills and Williamson 210; Spicer), ethnicity (Bosseaux; Potts; Ní Fhlainn 159–62) and roman-tic involvement with Buffy (Crawford 121–37; Dudek; Leon), only Laura Wright has analysed their diet. Her study is brief: she argues that *Buffy* fails to 'engage in any meaningful way with the politics of vampiric consump-tion of animals in the stead of humans' and that all Angel's and Spike's animal-blood diets '[are] indicative of is impotence' (48, 49). Nevertheless,

---

[1] Just how complex and perplexing *Buffy*'s engagement with dietary matters is can also be seen in its treatment of non-normative human diets. As Laura Wright notes, 'throughout *Buffy* there are few if any references to vegetarian[ism] or veganism that are not disparaging' (47). For example, in season two's 'I Only Have Eyes for You', when Billy Crandle chains himself to the snack machine off-screen, Principal Snyder responds by calling him a 'pathetic little no-life vegan' (00:06:21–27)—a quip that contains the first and only reference to veg-ans in the series. Snyder's intolerant attitude re-emerges in season six's 'Older and Far Away' when one of Buffy's co-workers from the Doublemeat Palace arrives at her birthday party only to tell the Scoobies that she 'can't have any chocolate ... or peanuts or egg yolks [or] dairy' (00:14:53–15:01). Owing to her dietary intolerances, she also 'can't really drink beer, 'cause you know, barley' (00:17:25–28). Her food intolerances are met with Anya's, Xander's and Willow's scorn.

[2] Works offering useful accounts of *Buffy* include Pateman; Pender; South, *Buffy the Vampire Slayer*; Stevenson; Wilcox and Lavery; and Wilcox, *Why Buffy Matters*. See also the *The International Journal of Buffy+'s* online scholarly journal *Slayage* and its undergraduate journal *Watcher Junior*.

her focus on two episodes (season three's 'The Wish' and season six's 'The Doublemeat Palace') in which *Buffy* engages 'tacitly' with the politics of meat consumption (49–51) is a good first step that sheds some light on the understudied dietary politics of *Buffy*.

Wright is not wrong when she claims that *Buffy* links its vampires' consumption of animal blood to impotence. However, I disagree with her claim that the series does not engage meaningfully with the politics of the animal-blood diet. In my view it does, even if not overtly or at great length (47). In particular, *Buffy* anticipates some aspects of the vegetarian vampire, which become important in later texts such as *Twilight* and *True Blood*. This is not to say that *Buffy* itself advances the trajectory of the vegetarian vampire, at least not to the extent that later fictions do. It is unable to do this, owing to the constraints of the slayer narrative, which shapes the show as a whole. Nevertheless, we find in *Buffy* key developments related to human-blood abstinence and the types of inter-species relationships that become more common in later, twenty-first-century vampire texts.

Magic, Microchips and Diet

Neither Angel nor Spike ever choose to adopt a diet of animal blood. Instead, abstention from human blood is forced upon them. Angel's abstinence is the (unintended) result of a gypsy curse that restored his soul, which is something that vampires lack. As Angel explains to Buffy, 'when you become a vampire, the demon takes your body, but it doesn't get your soul. That's gone! No conscience, no remorse … it's an easy way to live' ('Angel' 00:36:12–22). But the gypsy curse, by restoring his soul, also restores his conscience and ability to feel remorse: it therefore brings upon Angel an eternity of guilt and torment for all the lives he took as the blood-thirsty Angelus (his human-blood drinking alter-ego).[3] He therefore cannot bring himself to feed on or kill humans and subsists instead largely on pig's blood, although 'the show [rarely] alludes to his consumption at all' (Wright 48). As he tells Buffy, 'You have no idea what it's like to have done the things I've done, and to care. I haven't fed on a living human being since that day' ('Angel' 00:36:31–34).

---

[3] For an in-depth discussion of Angel and Angelus that takes into consideration their depiction on *Buffy* and its spin-off series *Angel*, see Abbott, 'Walking'; Kind; and Magnusson.

Angel's abstinence from human blood is therefore contingent on his curse, as is made clear by the events of *Buffy*'s second season, when Angel loses his soul after having sex with Buffy ('Innocence').[4] The effect of this loss is immediate: post-coitus, Angel becomes as wicked as any of *Buffy*'s vampires who have continued to imbibe human blood. Paraphrasing Sarah Owens, Wright argues that the curse is proof that in *Buffy* a diet of animal blood and vampiric impotence are closely linked: 'Angel, the "most sexualised and eroticized of all the characters" (Owens 27) cannot have sex or he will become Angelus' (49). Nevertheless, by having Angel's blood-abstinence and status-as-good contingent upon a curse, *Buffy* complicates the Ricean shift in characterisation that is opened up by the animal-blood diet, namely, that a vampire is not inherently evil but has a capacity for good. In *Interview*, that capacity largely stems from the free will and agency that Louis is shown to have, which enables him to make the choice to go against his vampiric nature and subsist on animal blood (at least for a time). Angel's curse, however, circumvents the act of choosing and, in so doing, narrows the extent to which Angel can be seen as good and moral (Crawford 125). Further, the rapidity with which Angel reverts to Angelus, who immediately begins again to torment and kill humans, suggests that Angel, when not constrained by something outside himself, does not consider drinking human blood to be wrong. Contrariwise, it suggests that Angelus and all he represents—in a word, evil—lurks beneath the surface of Angel, thus confirming again that it is only the curse that works to make Angel good. This suggests that in *Buffy* a vampire's conscience cannot operate outside the constraints imposed by magic.

Despite Buffy's faith in Angel, other characters, such as Kendra, who is a second slayer, and Ms Calender, realise the limits of Angel's conversion and 'never fully accept his having overcome vampire status' (Ono 172). However, neither the curse (nor *Buffy*) mandates that Angel *must* feed on animal blood. So, it would appear that Angel does make some sort of choice. He could still feed on human blood and, like Louis, attempt to suppress or merely endure the torment it intensifies. Instead, he chooses

[4] Critics have read Angel's reversion to Angelus, after having sex, as a metaphor for the pitfalls of teen sex Crawford 126; Ní Fhlainn 157; Stafford 168; and Taylor 42. Gall Berman, an executive producer on the show, claimed that 'we were not endorsing [teenage sex] or trivializing it. When Buffy and Angel have relations, it is not a good thing' (qtd. in Moy 86). The series revisits this trope in the season four episode 'The Harsh Light of Day', when Buffy sleeps with Parker, a co-ed at college, only to be rejected once again. For a contrary view on sex and sexuality in *Buffy*, see Nicol.

to subsist on animal blood and, unlike Louis, chooses to help protect humans from vampires (Hughes 240). We can therefore say that the link drawn in *Interview*, between a diet of animal rather than human blood and goodness, morality and care, is confirmed by Angel. But this link is also problematic. We can never say with certainty that Angel has become a good, animal-blood drinking vampire—Angelus seems always to lurk beneath Angel's actions.

Spike also never chooses to subsist on an animal-blood diet. On the contrary, from his first appearance in season two's 'School Hard', he thrives on a steady diet of humans—or 'happy meals with legs' ('Becoming: Part II' 00:09:35–37) as he dubs them—and is motivated by a singular desire to kill the slayer. Only in the fourth season, when Spike is captured by the Initiative, a government-sanctioned military operation tasked with the capture of, and research on, demons for military purposes, does his diet change ('The Initiative'). Dubbed 'Hostile 17' (00:41:53), Spike becomes a test subject for the Initiative's 'Behavioural-Modification Circuitry', a microchip that is implanted in the brain. This microchip prevents its demonic recipients from harming or attempting to harm 'in any way' any non-demonic life form, by ensuring that these actions are accompanied by 'intense neurological pain' (00:41:53–57). In Wright's view, Spike's microchip renders him impotent insofar as it prevents him from being able 'to kill humans' (49). However, Wright's assessment of Spike's microchip, like her account of Angel's animal-blood diet, is reductive and ignores its broader significance. Unlike Angel's curse, the microchip does not eliminate Spike's thirst for human blood. *Buffy* depicts Spike's predicament—his desire for human blood and inability to act on said desire—and the ensuing misery it brings him in 'Pangs', as he engages in voyeur-like behaviour, watching dejectedly through the window of an abandoned warehouse as other vampires feed on and kill a human. But with the microchip in place, Spike can no longer act on his still-intact urges. He bemoans this condition to Buffy, telling her 'it looks like they've done me for good … Spike's had a little trip to the vet, and now he doesn't chase the other puppies anymore. I can't bite anything—I can't even hit people!' (00:30:59–31:12). 'Stymied by the technology in his head' (Boyette, par. 12), he is forced to adopt a diet of animal blood. His decision to subsist on a diet of animal blood is therefore forced by the microchip rather than being a deliberate moral choice on his part. It is, therefore, uninformed by concern for human suffering.

Nevertheless, Spike's diet of pig's blood leads to a series of important changes in his character that confirm, in more certain terms than Angel's, what was first seen in *Interview*, namely, that when vampires shift from a diet of human to animal blood, they are able to develop sentience, including the ability to care for and love humans. These changes become apparent over the course of *Buffy*'s final seasons as, with the microchip implanted in his head, Spike becomes Buffy's and the Scoobies' (her friends and sidekicks) friend rather than foe, and a doer of good rather than evil—changes that ultimately lead Spike to regain what Louis believes he has lost and what Angel can never possess in his own right: a soul.[5] At first, these changes to Spike's character seem superficial, a matter of necessity, not unlike his decision to subsist on pig's blood. In order to eat, Spike needs money to purchase blood from the butcher's shop, so he swaps demonic intel for payment (a deal that Giles accepts in 'A New Man' but Buffy never stoops to).[6] This alliance gradually evolves in the fourth season to include Spike fighting alongside, rather than against, Buffy and the Scoobies. His actions here are again not tied to a change of heart: Spike joins in the fight only when he discovers that, because the chip only works on non-demonic life forms, he can hurt and harm other demons without repercussions for himself.[7] As Gert Magnusson points out, Spike fights demons 'because he relishes finally being able to fight again, not because of the good he is doing' (par. 12).[8] Spike's motivation—his desire to do and be good—only changes when he develops romantic feelings for Buffy ('Out of My Mind'), feelings that are the result of the shifts in interaction between Spike and Buffy that are made possible by the microchip and the animal-blood diet it enforces.

[5] There are negative aspects to Spike's efforts to regain a soul that discount the positive work of Spike's microchip. It seems to suggest, at the very least, that a vampire in the *Buffyverse* cannot ever be truly redeemed by any moral choice on their part. For more on this, see Crawford 130.

[6] She does, however, pay Spike to 'tell the tale' of how he killed two former slayers in hope of avoiding a similar fate ('Fool for Love' 00:10:30–11:30).

[7] The fact that Spike attempts to have the microchip removed in order to kill Buffy in the season five episode 'Out of My Mind', evinces the incremental nature of Spike's shift in characterisation from evil to good during the early period of his microchip.

[8] As David Lavery notes, Spike's eagerness to 'make use of his newly rediscovered power to kill demons' is evident in 'Doomed', where he eagerly suggests to Willow and Xander that 'we go out there and kick a little demon ass! … For justice—and for—the safety of puppies—and Christmas, right? Let's fight that evil! —Let's kill something!' (par. 24).

The microchip's ability to rewire Spike's character is important in light of its initial purpose: it is behaviour modification technology designed only to prevent Spike from harming humans. Although it achieves this purpose, the microchip goes beyond simply stymieing Spike's ability to feed on human blood. Instead, it 'guides him into re-humanization, a redeeming of the self',[9] and 'toward a soul, involuntarily or not; as Dawn points out in "Crush", soul or chip in the head—"same diff"' (Boyette, par. 17).[10] The sixth season episode 'Smashed' reveals as much when Spike, operating under the belief that his chip has stopped working, 'goes hunting for a human to eat' (Wilcox, *Why Buffy Matters* 88). But, as Rhonda Wilcox observes, 'when [Spike] chooses one, he seems to have to talk himself into the act with a diatribe of some length in front of his intended victim' (*Why Buffy Matters* 88): 'I know what I am. I'm dangerous. I'm evil. Yes, I am. I'm a killer. That's what I do. I kill. And yeah, maybe it's been a long time but it's not like you forget how. You just do it. And now I can. Again. Alright. So here goes' (00:17:08–35). What could have been a menacing speech in the hands of say, Angelus, is pitiable at best, and Spike concludes, as Wilcox notes, 'with an almost apology: "This might hurt a little"' (*Why Buffy Matters* 88).[11]

Buffy adds to rather than simply confirms some of the key elements of the animal-blood diet as established in *Interview*. The introduction of technology in the form of Spike's microchip, for example, signals the way in which the vampiric body can be changed (for the better) by technology. This is an important development, which prefigures later texts like *True Blood* and *The Southern Vampire Mysteries* that are built upon the biotechnological marvel of synthetic blood. Still more importantly, *Buffy* builds on the possibility of romantic relations between humans and those vampires who consume animal blood, as first intimated in *Interview*. Where

---

[9] There are hints, even before the chip is introduced, that Spike has always been 'a very human vampire' (Boyette, par. 9). In season two, for example, Spike is willing to help Buffy prevent Angelus from bringing about the apocalypse because he is fond of 'dog racing [and] Manchester United' ('Becoming Part II' 00:09:26–29). See Bailey and Boyette for further discussion.

[10] On this point Crawford disagrees, instead arguing that far from humanizing Spike, the microchip still allows him to 'hurt *something*', namely demons, which ultimately adheres to and therefore 'maintain[s] [*Buffy*'s structuring] principle that all vampires ... [are] inherently and irredeemably evil' (128).

[11] For an opposing view on a number of issues in this section related to Spike's microchip, see Bussolini 325–34 and Ní Fhlainn 158.

this is little more than a suggestion in *Interview*, in *Buffy* a degree of intimacy is allowed to unfurl between Buffy and Angel, and Buffy and Spike. Unlike Babette, Buffy reciprocates Angel's (and to a lesser degree, Spike's) feelings. In so doing, *Buffy* goes a step further than *Interview* and 'establishes, perhaps for the first time, the possibility of true coexistence, friendship, and (nonconsumptive) intimacy between … vampires and humans' (Wright 47). This intimacy, born from an animal-blood diet, is arguably the necessary first step towards realising the multispecies cohabiting, comingling and community that we see in later texts. As Debra Dudek observes, 'when Buffy falls in love with Angel and Angel with Buffy', 'a new syntax'—her term for the structural elements of a genre—'begins' (31).

While *Buffy* can be seen as precipitating 'an ideological and affective shift from fearing and/or sympathising with a vampire to loving him' (Dudek 31), it also places a limit on the extent to which intimacy between Buffy and Angel, and Buffy and Spike, can progress.[12] For Angel to be good requires that he remains celibate; but although celibacy is not an issue that Buffy and Spike contemplate, she nevertheless arrives at the conclusion that being intimate with him is 'wrong' ('Dead Things' 00:39:50–42:44).[13] There are, of course, other types of intimacy that *Buffy* explores. In early episodes of season six, for example, Spike becomes Buffy's closest confidante, and the two come to a deep understanding of each other. For instance, when Buffy is forced to drop out of college and work at The Doublemeat Palace (a fast-food restaurant that resembles McDonald's), only Spike discerns her despair and tells her 'this place will kill you' ('The Doublemeat Palace' 00:15:42–43). He also develops a close relationship with Buffy's sister, Dawn, vowing to protect her until his life or the world comes to an end ('Intervention' 00:42:27–31). Although romantic relationships between humans and vampires are not realised in *Buffy*, the fact that friendships do develop represents an important step towards a less destructive relation between these species.

---

[12] Crawford also arrives at this conclusion, noting that 'ultimately … *Buffy* is not a romance. There is no happy ending for Buffy and Spike, or for Buffy and Angel'. He even ventures to suggest that 'Buffy never really comes to love the monsters who court her enough to forgive them for their monstrous deeds' (134).

[13] Important essays on Buffy and Spike's relationship include Heinecken; Jowett 144–64; Larbalestier; Spah; and Symonds. See also Crawford 128–35.

BUFFY, SPECIES AND GENRE

In the world of *Buffy*, any approach to relations between humans and vampires must be tentative because it is centred on the vampire slayer. As James B. South writes, 'Buffy's purpose is simple enough: she is a vampire slayer' ('"All Torment"' 96) and her duty is to kill vampires and other demonic forces. According to Susan Owens, Buffy's purpose is announced by 'her name': she is the buffer between the human and the demonic world (25). How then could vampire-human relations develop while Buffy defends the border between human and vampire worlds? With the exception of Angel and Spike (and a handful of recurring vampires like Drusilla, Mr. Trick, The Master and Darla), the majority of vampires in *Buffy* are McGuffins: their time on screen is 'limited to brief, menacing appearances', which are often quoted in teasers, 'and capped with a spectacular death scene' (Benefiel 261).[14] This treats vampires as 'a uniform and persistent background menace over which Buffy consistently triumphs [rather] than as a kind of "other" suitable for psychological and social engagement' (Wright 47). Vampires also subscribe to this primal, binary logic. According to Spike, it is a vampire's duty to 'kill [the] Slayer, suck ... her dry, [and] pick ... his teeth with her bones'. It has, he adds, 'always been that way' ('Seeing Red' 00:33:10–18).[15] This primal conflict between a slayer and vampires makes it difficult for *Buffy* to bridge the human-vampire divide.[16]

Despite all this *Buffy* does take a few tentative steps that make the line between human and vampire worlds less straight-forward. As noted above, friendships do develop between Buffy and Angel, and Buffy and Spike. Just as importantly, it shows a slayer capable of feeling love for her enemy. This presents a radical challenge to the primal conflict that structures the series. As Joseph Crawford points out, 'the fact that such a storyline appeared at all in a fictional franchise so determinedly committed to the

[14] For an overview of the role of vampires in *Buffy*, see Ono 170 and Pateman 101–02.

[15] Spike maintains this position when he is confronted with the child of a previous slayer (whom he killed), telling her that 'I don't give a piss about your mum. She was a slayer. I was a vampire. That's the way the game is played' ('Lies My Parents Told Me' 00:35:03–11). In the fifth season episode 'Fool for Love', Spike puts the relationship between vampires and the slayer in less extreme terms, when he informs Buffy that 'to most vampires, the slayer [is] this object of cold sweat and frightened whispers' (00:22:51–57).

[16] According to Bruce McClelland, this conflict between the slayer and vampire extends back to the 'earliest folklore about vampires' (7). See *Slayers* for an in-depth discussion of the role of the slayer in folklore and history.

idea that monsters are both physically and morally monstrous' (130) is extremely significant, not least because it shows the binaries that *Buffy* is structured upon are less certain than previously thought. When Buffy discovers that Angel is a vampire and reveals the details of this to Giles and Xander, each repeats the logic that structures the series. Giles reminds her that killing Angel 'is the slayer's duty' ('Angel' 00:18:21–22). Xander puts the same imperative in more evolutionary terms when he states that 'fish gotta swim, birds gotta fly' (00:23:03–04). Both remind Buffy that the slayer is ideologically conservative rather than disruptive: vampires 'are there to be killed in the name of preserving things as they are' (McClelland 185). But Buffy rejects their thinking and pursues Angel. She also later pursues Spike, even though she knows—and others tell her—that it is wrong.[17]

According to Hilary M. Leon, Buffy's role as a slayer enables *Buffy* to explore romantic relations between vampire and slayer. As she explains, Buffy's role means that she spends 'more time, and share[s] more emotionally charged experiences, with [her] future [vampire] lovers than with any human males' (par. 20). Further, vampires can become partners 'who can fight alongside [her], ... whose safety is not a constant cause for concern' (par. 21). Because vampires know she is the slayer, she does not need to hide her identity from them (par. 24). What Leon does not consider, however, is that Buffy is also part demon, as is revealed in the seventh season, when Buffy discovers that the body of the first slayer was infused with the spirit of a demon, 'deliberately constructing a human/demon hybrid as humanity's protector from monsters' (Abbott, *Undead Apocalypse* 120). While proximity, physicality and honesty no doubt provide the conditions in which Buffy's attraction to Angel (and Spike) can grow, her divided genetic inheritance helps explain why this attraction is possible (and yet unable fully to be realised). Buffy is mid-way between human and demonic worlds, with vampires being a prominent part of the latter. In later texts like *Twilight*, *The Vampire Diaries* and *True Blood* it becomes possible to entertain serious human-vampire relationships which, like the one that develops between Edward and Bella, can culminate in

---

[17] In season four's 'Something Blue' for example, a spell causes Buffy and Spike to get engaged. Unaware of this, Giles calls Willow for help, telling her 'something has gone wrong ... horribly wrong' in reference to Buffy's and Spike's affectionate display (00:24:44–58). Even Spike concludes that his feelings for Buffy are 'wrong' ('Crush' 00:39:55–40:02).

marriage. In contrast to *Buffy*, these texts are not centred on a vampire slayer, and so the human-vampire divide is quarantined from the primal, ritualistic, and duty-bound conflicts that inform *Buffy*.

As I have been suggesting, if *Buffy* portrayed vampires as capable of choosing not to feed on human blood, the series as a whole would have to change. A world in which vampires are capable of living amongst and caring for humans would be a world in which the slayer is no longer necessary. It is fascinating, therefore, that a slayer-less Sunnydale is exactly what season three's episode 'The Wish' depicts, which is the result of Cordelia's (unknowing) wish, addressed to a vengeance demon, that 'Buffy Summers never came to Sunnydale' (00:15:00–04). In the alternate universe this creates, Buffy has been slaying in Cleveland, where, according to Giles, 'there is a great deal of demonic activity' (00:27:13–17). As a result, Sunnydale is now ruled by vampires (with Willow and Xander now amongst their throng). In this 'rather grim' Sunnydale (South, '"All Torment"' 96), there are after-dark curfews, monthly memorials for the dead, and everyone wears black because they know that 'vampires are attracted to bright colours' (00:21:14–17). But most notable of all, this Sunnydale is home to The Master (whom Giles refers to as the 'vampire king' ['Out of Mind, Out of Sight' 00:17:00]) and his factory, the first of its kind, in which blood is harvested from captive humans. 'The Wish' therefore confirms the need for a slayer and also that (with Angel and Spike as the exceptions) 'most vampires are still evil monsters who have to die' (Dudek 31). Both are confirmed in unusually unequivocal form when Buffy appears late in the episode, after having been contacted by Giles. In order to reinstate the proper boundary between worlds, Buffy 'fights ... with few kicks, no creativity, and a ramrod straight posture'—'it's just "plunge and move on", as Giles urges her in "Never Kill a Boy on the First Date"' (Kociemba, par. 13).

While 'The Wish' exaggerates the propensity for violence and inherent wickedness of vampires, it also suggests that on one point the two species are the same. This is established by the episode's focus on factory farms (Pateman 77) and on the relation between eater and eaten.[18] Starting with the former, the similarities between The Master's factory farm and our own practices of factory farming are apparent in the plant's mise-en-scene. The first, like the second, is replete with conveyer belts, health and safety signage, and workers wearing hard hats. If one puts animals in the place of

[18] For a counterpoint, see South, '"All Torment"' 97.

humans and humans in the place of vampires, The Master's factory seems still more familiar. In the vampire's factory farm, humans (like cattle in our factory farms), 'are herded', kept in pens, and 'stunned' ('with … cattle prod[s]') before being loaded onto a conveyer belt (Wright 49). The next step is, of course, different: the vampires drain the humans of their blood 'via metal implements that are inserted into their bodies at various points' (Wright 49), whereas humans send cattle to the abattoirs. Wright finds it notable that 'the initial victim is female' (50) and argues that this choice alludes to our rearing of female cows for the purposes of milk. She writes:

> the implements that pierce the flesh of this first female victim evoke, in their shape and function, the electronic machinery used in the industrial milking of cows and highlight the connection of vampiric blood drinking and human consumption of factory-farmed cow's milk. (50)

However, 'The Wish' also draws a parallel between blood-drinking and meat-eating, which appears when viewers realise that humans and vampires both depend on (and destroy) the bodies of supposedly lesser beings for nourishment (Del Principe 25). The female victim is, as Wright observes, 'ultimately [drained] … to death so that The Master can drink her blood from a wine glass' (50). Animals also ultimately die so that we can consume their meat. As The Master proclaims at the plant's grand opening, 'death is our art' (00:37:14–16). But as this episode points out, death is our art too. What 'The Wish' thus draws attention to is the real-world reality that 'the allegedly evil actions of vampires'—in feeding on and killing humans—'differ not one scintilla from what we ourselves do all the time to [non-human animals]' (Blayde and Dunn 42).

These parallels between humans and vampires can be entertained only temporarily, created when Cordelia's wish is granted and terminated when, in the episode's final moments, Giles destroys its power source, the vengeance demon's necklace. Sunnydale then 'snaps back to its "normal" state … and history is repaired' (Westerfield 39). In the context of *Buffy*, a return to normal is a return to the primal logic of the slayer, which keeps the categories of human and vampire separate and distinct. Once again, the logic of the series can be suspended only with the help of an outside force, in this case magic, which allows parallels between humans and vampires to be explored, but also for the 'normal' world of *Buffy* to eventually be reinstated.

Notwithstanding the constraints of the genre to which *Buffy* belongs, it is, unlike *Interview*, able to imagine a world in which vampires, as represented by Angel and Spike, can help (and protect) Buffy, and even emerge as 'defenders of humanity' (Hughes 240). Limited by the constraints of the slayer narrative, *Buffy* can explore from time to time but ultimately not bridge the gap between humans and vampires. It can be said, then, that *Buffy* sets down a challenge to later vampire texts by clearly showing both its own Manichean limits and the way beyond them. How *Twilight*, *The Vampire Diaries* and *True Blood* take up these challenges is the subject of the next chapters.

Works Cited

Abbott, Stacey. *Undead Apocalypse: Vampires and Zombies in the 21ˢᵗ Century.* Edinburgh UP, 2016. *JSTOR*, www.jstor.org/stable/10.3366/j.cttlg050nn.

———. 'Walking the Fine Line Between Angel and Angelus.' *Slayage: The International Journal of Buffy+*, vol. 3, no. 1, Aug. 2003, www.whedonstudies. tv/uploads/2/6/2/8/26288593/abbott_slayage_3.1.pdf.

Bailey, Joseph Doherty. '"Newly Human and Strangely Literal": Embodiments of Haraway's Simian, Cyborg, and Woman in *Buffy the Vampire Slayer.*' *Watcher Junior: The Undergraduate Journal of Buffy+*, vol. 8, no. 1, spring 2015, www. whedonstudies.tv/uploads/2/6/2/8/26288593/bailey_watcherjunior_ 8.1.pdf.

Benefiel, Candace R. 'Blood Relations: The Gothic Perversion of the Nuclear Family in Anne Rice's *Interview with the Vampire.*' *Journal of Popular Culture*, vol. 38, no. 2, 2004, pp. 261–73. *Wiley Online Library*, https://doi. org/10.1111/j.0022-3840.2004.00111.x.

Bosseaux, Charlotte. '"Bloody Hell. Sodding, Blimey, Shagging, Knickers, Bollocks. O' God, I'm English": Translating Spike.' *Gothic Studies*, vol. 15, no. 1, pp. 21–32. *Edinburgh UP*, https://doi.org/10.7227/GS.15.1.3.

Boyette, Michele. 'The Comic Anti-Hero in *Buffy the Vampire Slayer*, or Silly Villain: Spike is for Kicks.' *Slayage: The International Journal of Buffy+*, vol. 1, no. 4, Dec. 2001, www.whedonstudies.tv/uploads/2/6/2/8/26288593/ boyette_slayage_1.4.pdf.

Bussolini, Jeffrey. 'Technology and Magic: Joss Whedon's Explorations of the Mind.' Wilcox et al., pp. 325–40.

Chandler, Holly. 'Slaying the Patriarchy: Transfusions of the Vampire Metaphor in *Buffy the Vampire Slayer.*' *Slayage: The International Journal of Buffy+*, vol. 3, no. 1, Aug. 2003, www.whedonstudies.tv/uploads/2/6/2/8/26288593/ chandler_slayage_3.1.pdf.

Crawford, Joseph. *The Twilight of the Gothic? Vampire Fiction and the Rise of the Paranormal Romance*. Wales UP, 2014. *JSTOR*, www.jstor.org/stable/j. ctt9qhjcp.

Del Principe. '(M)eating Dracula: Food and Death in Stoker's Novel.' *Gothic Studies*, vol. 16, no. 1, May 2014, pp. 24–38. *Edinburgh UP*, https://doi. org/10.7227/GS.16.1.3.

Dudek, Debra. *The Beloved Does Not Bite: Moral Vampires and the Humans Who Love Them*. Routledge, 2018. *Taylor and Francis Online*, https://doi. org/10.4324/9781315225425.

Erickson, Gregory. 'From Old Heresies to Future Paradigms: Joss Whedon on Body and Soul.' Wilcox et al., pp. 341–55.

Heinecken, Dawn. 'Fan Readings of Sex and Violence on *Buffy the Vampire Slayer*.' *Slayage: The International Journal of Buffy+*, vol. 3, no. 3–4, Apr. 2004, www.whedonstudies.tv/uploads/2/6/2/8/26288593/heinecken_slayage_3.3-4.pdf.

Hills, Matt, and Rebecca Williamson. '*Angel*'s Monstrous Mothers and Vampires with Souls: Investigating the Abject in "Television Horror."' *Reading Angel: The TV Spin-Off with a Soul*, edited by Stacey Abbott, I.B. Tauris, 2005, pp. 203–17.

Hughes, James. 'Posthumans and Democracy in Popular Culture.' *The Palgrave Handbook of Posthumanism in Film and Television*, edited by Michael Hauskeller et al., Palgrave Macmillan, 2015, pp. 235–45. *Springer Link*, https://doi. org/10.1057/9781137430328.

Jowett, Lorna. *Sex and the Slayer: A Gender Studies Primer for the Buffy Fan*. Wesleyan UP, 2005.

Kind, Amy. 'The Vampire with a Soul: Angel and the Quest for Identity.' *The Philosophy of Horror*, edited by Thomas Fahy, Kentucky UP, 2010, pp. 86–101. *JSTOR*, www.jstor.org/stable/j.ctt2jck39.

Kociemba, David. '"Where's the fun?": The Comic Apocalypse in "The Wish."' *Slayage: The International Journal of Buffy+*, vol. 6, no. 3, spring 2007, www. whedonstudies.tv/uploads/2/6/2/8/26288593/kociemba_slayage_6.3.pdf.

Larbalestier, Justine. 'The Only Thing Better Than Killing A Slayer: Heterosexuality and Sex in *Buffy The Vampire Slayer*.' *Reading the Vampire Slayer: The New Updated, Unofficial Guide to Buffy and Angel*, edited by Roz Kaveney, 2nd ed., and expanded, Tauris Parke, 2004, pp. 195–219.

Lavery, David. 'Apocalyptic Apocalypses: The Narrative Eschatology of *Buffy the Vampire Slayer*.' *Slayage: The International Journal of Buffy+*, vol. 3, no. 1, Aug. 2003, www.whedonstudies.tv/uploads/2/6/2/8/26288593/lavery_slayage_3.1.pdf.

Leon, Hilary M. 'Why We Love the Monsters: How Anita Blake, Vampire Hunter, and Buffy the Vampire Slayer Wound Up Dating the Enemy.' *Slayage: The International Journal of Buffy+*, vol. 1, no. 1, Jan. 2001, www.whedonstudies. tv/uploads/2/6/2/8/26288593/leon_slayage_1.1.pdf.

Magnusson, Gert. 'Are Vampires Evil? Categorizations of Vampires, and Angelus and Spike as the Immoral and the Amoral.' *Slayage: The International Journal of Buffy+*, vol. 9, no. 2, fall 2012, www.whedonstudies.tv/uploads/2/6/2/8/26288593/magnusson_2__slayage_9.2.pdf.

McClelland, Bruce. *Slayers and Their Vampires: A Cultural History of Killing the Dead*. Michigan UP, 2006. *JSTOR*, www.jstor.org/stable/10.3998/mpub.22395.

McLaren, Scott. 'The Evolution of Joss Whedon's Vampire Mythology and the Ontology of the Soul.' *Slayage: The International Journal of Buffy+*, vol. 2, no. 5, Sept. 2005, www.whedonstudies.tv/uploads/2/6/2/8/26288593/mclaren_slayage_5.2.pdf.

Moy, Suelain. 'Girls Who Fight Back.' *Good Housekeeping*, vol. 228, no. 4, Apr. 1999, p. 86.

Nicol, Rhonda. '"When You Kiss Me, I Want To Die": Arrested Feminism in *Buffy the Vampire Slayer* and the *Twilight* Series.' *Bringing Light to Twilight: Perspectives on the Pop Culture Phenomenon*, edited by Giselle Liza Anatol, Palgrave Macmillan, 2011, pp. 113–23.

Ní Fhlainn, Sorcha. *Postmodern Vampires: Film, Fiction, and Popular Culture*. Palgrave Macmillan, 2019. *Springer Link*, https://doi.org/10.1057/978-1-137-58377-2.

Ono, Kent. 'To Be a Vampire on Buffy the Vampire Slayer: Race and ("Other") Socially Marginalizing Positions on Horror TV.' *Fantasy Girls: Gender in the New Universe of Sci-Fi and Fantasy T.V*, edited by Elyse Rae Helford, Rowman and Littlefield, 2000, pp. 163–86.

Owens, Susan A. 'Vampires, Postmodernity and Postfeminism: Buffy the Vampire Slayer.' *Journal of Popular Film and Television*, vol. 27, 1999, pp. 24–31. *Taylor and Francis Online*, https://doi.org/10.1080/01956059909602801.

Pateman, Matthew. *The Aesthetics of Culture in Buffy the Vampire Slayer*. McFarland, 2006.

Pender, Patricia. *I'm Buffy and You're History: Buffy the Vampire Slayer and Contemporary Feminism*. I.B. Tauris, 2016.

Potts, Donna L. 'Convents, Claddagh Rings, and Even *The Book of Kells*: Representing the Irish in *Buffy the Vampire Slayer*.' *Simile: Students in Media and Information Literacy Education*, vol. 2, no. 3, May 2003, pp. 1–9, https://doi.org/10.3138/sim.3.2.002.

South, James B. '"All Torment, Trouble, Wonder, and Amazement Inhabits Here": The Vicissitudes of Technology in *Buffy the Vampire Slayer*.' *Journal of American and Comparative Cultures*, vol. 24, no. 1–2, 2001, pp. 93–102. *ProQuest*, www.proquest.com/docview/200674525?accountid=12372.

———. editor. *Buffy the Vampire Slayer and Philosophy: Fear and Trembling in Sunnydale*. Open Court, 2003.

Spah, Victoria. '"Ain't Love Grand?" Spike and Courtly Love.' *Slayage: The International Journal of Buffy+*, vol. 2, no. 1, May 2002, www.whedonstudies.tv/uploads/2/6/2/8/26288593/spah_slayage_2.1.pdf.

Spicer, Arwen. "'Love's Bitch but Man Enough to Admit It": Spike's Hybridized Gender.' *Slayage: The International Journal of Buffy+*, vol. 2, no. 3, Dec. 2002, www.whedonstudies.tv/uploads/2/6/2/8/26288593/spicer_slayage_2.3.pdf.

Stafford, Nikki. *Bite Me! The Unofficial Guide to the World of Buffy the Vampire Slayer*. ECW Press, 2007.

Stevenson, Gregory. *Televised Morality: The Case of Buffy the Vampire Slayer.* Hamilton Books, 2003.

Symonds, Gwyn. "'Solving Problems with Sharp Objects": Female Empowerment, Sex and Violence in *Buffy the Vampire Slayer*.' *Slayage: The International Journal of Buffy+*, vol. 3, no. 3–4, Apr. 2004, www.whedonstudies.tv/uploads/2/6/2/8/26288593/symonds_slayage_3.3-4.pdf.

Taylor, Anthea. 'The Urge Towards Love Is an Urge Towards (Un)death: Romance, Masochistic Desire and Postfeminism in the *Twilight* Novels.' *International Journal of Cultural Studies*, vol. 15, no. 1, 2012, pp. 31–46. *Sage Journals*, https://doi.org/10.1177/1367877911399204.

Westerfield, Scott. 'A Slayer Comes to Town.' *Seven Seasons of Buffy: Science Fiction and Fantasy Authors Discuss Their Favourite Television Show*, edited by Glenn Yeffeth, BenBella Books, 2009, pp. 30–40. *ProQuest Ebook Central*, ebookcentral.proquest.com/lib/unimelb/detail.action?docID=909505.

Wilcox, Rhonda V. 'There Will Never Be a "Very Special" Buffy: *Buffy* and the Monsters of Teen Life.' *Journal of Popular Film and Television*, vol. 27, no. 2, summer 1999, pp. 16–23. *Taylor and Francis Online*, https://doi.org/10.1080/01956059909602800.

———. *Why Buffy Matters: The Art of Buffy the Vampire Slayer.* I.B. Tauris, 2005.

Wilcox, Rhonda V, and David Lavery, editors. *Fighting the Forces: What's at Stake in Buffy the Vampire Slayer.* Rowman and Littlefield, 2002.

Wilcox, Rhonda V., et al, editors. *Reading Joss Whedon.* Syracuse UP, 2014. *JSTOR*, www.jstor.org/stable/j.ctt1j2n7v0.

Wright, Laura. *The Vegan Studies Project: Food, Animals, and Gender in the Age of Terror.* Georgia UP, 2015. *JSTOR*, www.jstor.org/stable/j.ctt183q3vb.

TV

'Angel.' Directed by Scott Brazil. *Buffy the Vampire Slayer*, season 1, episode 7, The WB, 14 Apr. 1997. *Stan*, https://www.stan.com.au/.

'Becoming: Part II.' Directed by Joss Whedon. *Buffy the Vampire Slayer*, season 2, episode 21, The WB, 19 May 1997. *Stan*, https://www.stan.com.au/.

'Crush.' Directed by Dan Attias. *Buffy the Vampire Slayer*, season 5, episode 14, The WB, 13 Feb. 2001. *Stan*, https://www.stan.com.au/.

'Dead Things.' Directed by James A. Contner. *Buffy the Vampire Slayer*, season 6, episode 13, UPN, 5 Feb. 2002. *Stan*, https://www.stan.com.au/.

'Doomed.' Directed by James A. Contner. *Buffy the Vampire Slayer*, season 4, episode 11, The WB, 18 Jan. 2000. *Stan*, https://www.stan.com.au/.

'The Double Meat Palace.' Directed by Nick Marck. *Buffy the Vampire Slayer*, season 6, episode 12, UPN, 29 Jan. 2002. *Stan*, https://www.stan.com.au/.

'Fool for Love.' Directed by Nick Marck. *Buffy the Vampire Slayer*, season 5, episode 7, The WB, 14 Nov. 2000. *Stan*, https://www.stan.com.au/.

'The Harsh Light of Day.' Directed by James A. Contner. *Buffy the Vampire Slayer*, season 4, episode 3, The WB, 19 Oct. 1999. *Stan*, https://www.stan.com.au/.

'I Only Have Eyes for You.' Directed by James Whitmore, Jr. *Buffy the Vampire Slayer*, season 2, episode 19, The WB, 28 Apr. 1997. *Stan*, https://www.stan.com.au/.

'The Initiative.' Directed by James A. Contner. *Buffy the Vampire Slayer*, season 4, episode 7, The WB, 16 Nov. 1999. *Stan*, https://www.stan.com.au/.

'Innocence.' Directed by Joss Whedon. *Buffy the Vampire Slayer*, season 2 episode 14, The WB, 20 Jan. 1997. *Stan*, https://www.stan.com.au/.

'Intervention.' Directed by Michael Gershman. *Buffy the Vampire Slayer*, season 5, episode 18, The WB, 24 Apr. 2001. *Stan*, https://www.stan.com.au/.

'Lies My Parents Told Me.' Directed by David Fury. *Buffy the Vampire Slayer*, season 7, episode 17, UPN, 25 Mar. 2003. *Stan*, https://www.stan.com.au/.

'A New Man.' Directed by Michael Gershman. *Buffy the Vampire Slayer*, season 4, episode 12, The WB, 25 Jan. 2000. *Stan*, https://www.stan.com.au/.

'Older and Far Away.' Directed by Michael Gershman. *Buffy the Vampire Slayer*, season 6, episode 14, UPN, 12 Feb. 2002. *Stan*, https://www.stan.com.au/.

'Out of Mind, Out of Sight.' Directed by Reza Badiyi. *Buffy the Vampire Slayer*, season 1, episode 11, The WB, 19 May 1997. *Stan*, https://www.stan.com.au/.

'Out of My Mind.' Directed by David Grossman. *Buffy the Vampire Slayer*, season 5, episode 4, The WB, 17 Oct. 2000. *Stan*, https://www.stan.com.au/.

'Pangs.' Directed by Michael Lange. *Buffy the Vampire Slayer*, season 4, episode 8, The WB, 23 Nov. 1999. *Stan*, https://www.stan.com.au/.

'School Hard.' Directed by John T. Kretchmer. *Buffy the Vampire Slayer*, season 2, episode 3, The WB, 29 Nov. 1997. *Stan*, https://www.stan.com.au/.

'Seeing Red.' Directed by Michael Gershman. *Buffy the Vampire Slayer*, season 6, episode 19, UPN, 7 May 2002. *Stan*, https://www.stan.com.au/.

'Smashed.' Directed by Turi Meyer. *Buffy the Vampire Slayer*, season 6, episode 9, UPN, 20 Nov. 2001. *Stan*, https://www.stan.com.au/.

'Something Blue.' Directed by Nick Marck. *Buffy the Vampire Slayer*, season 4, episode 9, The WB, 30 Nov. 1999. *Stan*, https://www.stan.com.au/.

'The Wish.' Directed by David Greenwalt. *Buffy the Vampire Slayer*, season 3, episode 9, The WB, 8 Dec. 1998. *Stan*, https://www.stan.com.au/.

CHAPTER 4

Vegetarian Vampires: *Twilight*, Sustainability and Salvation

Abstract This chapter focuses on Stephenie Meyer's *Twilight* saga, arguing that it re-imagines the vampire's animal-blood diet in ways that make it environmentally conscious and attuned to contemporary concerns, expressed in particular by modern vegetarianism, about animal welfare and the environmental damage caused by a meat-based diet. The first part of this chapter highlights the ways in which *Twilight* explores possibilities opened by an animal-blood diet that were anticipated but not realised in *Interview* and *Buffy*. It also considers innovations made by Meyer to heighten the Cullens' moral character. The second part describes the ways in which the saga engages with contemporaneous ecological concerns. Attention is paid to the Cullens' hunting habits, feeding routine and conservation efforts, as well as the saga's salvation narrative. The latter is not symptomatic of Meyer's Mormonism, as is commonly argued; instead, it is taken here to be an allegory for human-earth relations in the Anthropocene.

Keywords Animal-blood diet • *Twilight* • Edward Cullen • Vegetarian • Vampires

S. Dungan, *Reading the Vegetarian Vampire*, Palgrave Gothic, https://doi.org/10.1007/978-3-031-18350-8_4

In Stephenie Meyer's *Twilight Saga* (2005–08),[1] we encounter a significantly revised human-blood abstinent vampire, one that updates, for a new age and ecological era, the nascent ethics and implications of the animal-blood diet that was introduced in *Interview* and then elaborated in *Buffy*. Set in a small town called Forks in Northwest Washington, near the Olympic ranges, the four-volume saga follows the developing relationship between the 17-year-old human protagonist (and later vampire), Bella Swan, and her boyfriend (and later husband), Edward Cullen, who like other members of his family is a vampire. Luckily for Bella, Edward and his family choose not to feed on humans; instead, they feed exclusively on animal blood, preying on large animals in the surrounding Olympic ranges (deer, elk, mountain lions and grizzly bears) to meet their blood needs. This diet makes the Cullens, as they joke, 'vegetarian' (*Twilight* 164) and enables them to assimilate into human society. Carlisle (their patriarch) works as a doctor at the local hospital, and his adopted children (as they pretend to be)—Edward, Emmett, Rosalie, Jasper and Alice—are students at the local high school. And not only do the Cullens not feed on humans, they are willing to defend humans against vampires who do, like James, Victoria, and Laurent.

The saga makes explicit the developments made possible by an animal-blood diet that were anticipated but not realised in *Interview* and *Buffy*. Romantic relationships between humans and vegetarian vampires ensue, with the latter able to not just to watch or love humans from afar, but to live amongst them, attend their schools and work in their hospitals. The saga also proposes that a change of diet can radically alter a species' relationship with other species. As Edward informs Bella, 'only those like us, who've given up hunting you people can live together with humans for any length of time' (*Twilight* 254). The case is made more expansively by Eleazar, the head of the saga's other vegetarian clan (the Denalis), who remarks that 'abstaining from human blood makes [vampires] more civilized' (*Breaking Dawn* 603).

The saga confirms this distinction between civilized and uncivilized vampires through its depiction of vampires who continue to consume human blood. Some vampires want to make Bella (and the human

---

[1] A fifth novel, *Midnight Sun*, a retelling of *Twilight* from Edward's perspective, was released on August 4, 2020. *Midnight Sun* is independent of the saga and so for this reason can be left safely outside the purview of this chapter. However, it is worth noting Edward's perspective offers no further insight to his diet.

population of Forks) a 'snack' (*Twilight* 331) and, as such, are categorized as uncivilized and therefore 'evil'. In book one, the uncivilized vampires include James, Victoria and Laurent, who roam through the Cullens' territory. To these vampires, Bella is nothing but a meal. They choose to ignore Carlisle's claim that Bella is 'with us' (*Twilight* 331) and, therefore, not on the menu, and opt instead to hunt her. In the second novel, the role of uncivilized or 'evil' vampire falls to members of the Volturi—the vampire royal authority—who not only subsist on human blood but have a long history of trying to curb Carlisle's aversion to his 'natural food source' (*Twilight* 297). Like James, Victoria and Laurent, they have no 'respect' for and do not trust human life (Gerhards 242), decreeing that Bella must become a vampire or die in order to protect their secret existence (*New Moon* 477–79). Conversely, the Cullens' animal-blood diet makes them civilized and therefore 'good', a feature registered by their golden eyes—which differ from the sinister red eyes of the 'evil' vampires who consume human blood (Gerhards 254–55; Kane 106–09; Leavenworth and Isaksson 167; Piatti-Farnell 22)—and by their constant struggle against their thirst for human blood.[2] Edward, for example, briefly leaves Forks to avoid the scent of Bella's blood, which he claims is like his 'own personal brand of heroin' (*Twilight* 234); and a single drop of blood, the result of a papercut, is sufficient for Jasper, the newest vegetarian, to lose control and attack Bella (*New Moon* 28–31).

The Cullens must struggle with their thirst for human blood because animal blood is a nutritionally inferior substitute for human blood, which does not properly quench their thirst. As Edward tells Bella, animal blood 'doesn't completely satiate the hunger—or rather thirst', it just 'keeps us strong enough to resist' (*Twilight* 164). This is in stark contrast to *Interview*'s and *Buffy*'s depiction of animal blood. Louis and Lestat never refer to animal blood's nutritional value, poor or otherwise. Lestat bemoans only the rapidity with which rat's blood gets cold (33), making it a less palatable option than human blood. Likewise in *Buffy*, there is no mention of animal blood's nutritional value: Angel barely mentions his consumption of pig's blood; and Spike (like Lestat), ignoring its nutritional value, quips that animal blood '"doesn't rank [high] in the Zagat Guide" [which rates the best restaurants in the world]' ('Something Blue' 00:07:17–19; Wright 49). As for later vampires, in *The Southern Vampire*

---

[2] Catherine Spooner registers the distinction between civilized and uncivilized vampires elsewhere, on Meyer's use of costume (153–54). See her article.

Mysteries, the type of blood does not appear to be particularly significant, at least not in itself. Although vampires enjoy synthetic blood for its taste (Sookie tells us that 'Bill had always enjoyed it'), 'flavour wasn't the thing; it was the sensation of biting into flesh, feeling the heartbeat of the human, that [makes drinking blood] fun' (*All Together Dead* 77). Only in *The Vampire Diaries* is there a mention of animal blood's inferiority, in nutritional terms, to human blood. Vampires who feed on animal blood find their strength and supernatural powers are diminished.

This innovation allows Meyer to heighten the Cullens' moral character by emphasising the degree of asceticism, discipline and control needed to refuse human blood. This struggle to abstain from human blood is not seen in *Interview* and *Buffy*. Angel struggles with his conscience, not his diet. And Spike, who is not all that bloodthirsty to begin with, is primarily driven by an 'ordinary lust for destruction' (Magnusson, par. 11): 'I liked the rush. I liked the crunch. Never did look back at the victims' ('Damage' 00:41:21–28; Magnusson, par. 11). Similarly, the vampires in *The Vampire Diaries* and *True Blood* do not struggle with their bloodlust (whether or not they decide to control it is another question). The only exception to this is Stefan, who belongs to a category of vampires known as 'rippers' ('The Dinner Party' 00:16:01)—vampires who have no control over their bloodthirst. But even his struggle is different from the Cullens'. Stefan's battle against his desire to consume human blood is the result of a genetic anomaly (his mother, Lily, is also a ripper) rather than a cosmic battle, centred on the vampire's diet, between good and evil. So, we can say with some certainty that the saga takes *Interview*'s and *Buffy*'s nascent dietary ethics and makes them overt. Vampires can be good, and they can love and live with humans, but only if they choose to subsist on a diet of animal blood. The ways in which the saga draws on and further develops the implications of innovations found in earlier texts is the subject of this chapter.

GOING GREEN: VEGETARIAN VAMPIRES AND THE ANTHROPOCENE

Critics have addressed the Cullens' vegetarianism through ecocritical (Mc Elroy and Mc Elroy 82; McFarland-Taylor 143–52; Parmiter 226), historicist (Buttsworth 52–54; Liedl 158–61), religious (Branch; Shaw 229–31; Toscano), and philosophical (Kazez; J. McMahon 200–03) frameworks, and treated their diet as reflective of the saga's post-modern (Gerhards 249–56), post-secular (Branch) and posthuman (Nayar 126–54), as well as political (Ní Fhlainn 219) context.[3] It has even been read as a metaphor for eating disorders (Rosenberg), drug addiction (Frank 344) and manners (Spooner 151–52). The Cullens' vegetarianism has also been the source of much ridicule, with one critic finding their diet to be 'the most disturbing part of the [saga]—beyond a hundred-year-old man ... dating a teenage girl' (Bacon 47), as has its designation 'vegetarian', a source of tension for critics (Wright 55–56) and in online fan forums (McFarland-Taylor 149–50; Leavenworth and Isaksson 168).

Several critics have also written at length on the connection between the Cullen family's abstention from human blood and the saga's broader insistence on sexual abstinence. This is demonstrated by Edward's refusal to engage in pre-marital sex because he believes it will ruin his 'shot at heaven, or whatever there is after this life' (*Eclipse* 453). As Ashely Donnelly writes, the saga's 'emphasis on denial of both the sexual and the primal (blood and violence) goes well beyond the issue of basic moral order of which most blood abstinent vampires concern themselves' (181). It also goes beyond the moral order of 'most contemporary vampire fictions' (including those in this study), which 'are culturally located in a moment in which sex is not confined to marriage—even Sookie's traditional [and Southern] grandmother does not oppose pre-marital sex' (Smith 206). For critics such as Natalie Wilson, Christine Seifert and Anna Silver, Edward's insistence on sexual abstinence reflects the saga's celebration of 'strong, patriarchal dominance' (Donnelly 181) and champions the need to police female sexuality.[4] As Donnelly points out, Edward's decision to abstain from pre-marital sex 'not only controls his life choices, but Bella's as well'

---

[3] Useful accounts of *Twilight* include Anatol; Clarke and Osborn; Clayton and Harman; Click et al.; Housel and Wisnewski; Klonsky et al.; Larsson and Steiner; Parke and Wilson; Reagin; and Wilson, *Seduced by Twilight*.

[4] A large portion of the secondary criticism on *Twilight* reads the novels through a feminist lens. For a discussion of how the saga romanticises domestic abuse and patriarchal authority, see Miller; and Torkelson. On the saga's depiction of regressive gender roles, see Ames; Averill; Rocha; Whitton; and Williamson. For a reading of how the saga polices female sexuality by promoting abstinence, see also Donnelly; Kane; Seifert; and Silver; for a contrary view, see Bealer, Nicol, and Spooner. The claim that these books are anti-feminist is also often made on fan boards. See user Nuxi's comment, for example, www.fanpop.com/clubs/ critical-analysis-of-twilight/articles/29723/title/anti-feminism-bella-swan-illusion-choice. In response, Meyer has defended her work as not at all anti-feminist on her website (stepheniemeyer.com/the-books/breaking-dawn/frequently-asked-questions-breaking-dawn/).

(181), and this amounts to control of Bella's body too: 'she is absolutely dependent on Edward's ability to protect her life, her virginity, and her humanity' (Seifert 25) even as his presence threatens each of these things.[5]

While there is merit in these discussions, they nevertheless ignore and downplay the ethical undercurrent of Edward's and his family's decision to abstain from their natural food source, namely, human blood, while being close to other interpretations of their diet's religious overtone. These readings are also blind to context, namely, the changing social and environmental conditions of the Anthropocene. This chapter argues that, in her four-volume saga, Stephenie Meyer ushers in what could be called an environmentally conscious or 'green' (McFarland-Taylor 2, 144) take on the vampire's animal-blood diet, one that is highly attuned to the concerns reflected by modern vegetarian diets, which stem ultimately from our ecological era. Nowadays, a vegetarian diet is driven predominantly by concerns for animal welfare and the environmental damage caused by a meat-based diet, with the second intensifying the first. We find these concerns refracted in Meyer's formulation of a (vampiric) vegetarian practice that is guided by a desire to protect humans, based apparently on their right to not be fed on, and by environmental considerations.

This concern is evident in the Cullen family's hunting methods. When they are not feeding on the abundance of local 'deer and elk' in the surrounding Olympic Ranges, they hunt seasonal[6] fare—'early spring is Emmett's favourite bear season', Edward tells Bella, as 'they're just coming out of hibernation, so they're more irritable'.[7] They also hunt exclusively in 'areas with an overpopulation of predators—ranging as far away as we need' (*Twilight* 188). These habits (hunting predators, as well as deer and elk) highlight the extent of the Cullens' desire to protect the environment (Leavenworth and Isaksson 167). By feeding on the abundance of deer and elk in the Olympic Ranges, the Cullens control as they cull the local 'population of foraging animals'. They likewise check the

---

[5] The saga's condemnation of pre-marital sex can also be seen in Meyer's description of pre-marital sex, which are always violent. In *Eclipse*, for example, it is revealed that a then-human Rosalie was raped by her fiancé, Royce and his friends, leading to her death (159–62), and there are hints in *Twilight* that a then-human Alice was sexually assaulted by an old vampire who coveted her.

[6] In this manuscript, environmental sustainability as a concept refers to the actions, practices, or efforts of individuals to mitigate or minimise their impact on the natural environment, as well as efforts to conserve nature and the natural environment.

[7] The Cullen family are, therefore, also 'locavores': people (vampires, in this case) who, 'in addition to being vegetarian or vegan, and sometimes neither, try to eat local, seasonal foods whenever possible' (Preece 17).

overpopulation of predators that would otherwise upset a 'well-balanced ecosystem' (Parmiter 29n232, 226). Edward puts this desire in more certain terms when he tells Bella that he and his family '*have* to be careful not to impact the environment with injudicious hunting' (*Twilight* 188; emphasis added). In comments like this, coupled with the Cullens' mindful eating practices, one can discern a sense of obligation to the natural world and its ecosystems not seen in earlier texts.

This awareness is certainly different from the vegetarian ethic espoused in *Interview* (and to a lesser extent, *Buffy*), which only concerns the right of humans to not be fed on. In *Interview*, Louis has no qualms about killing animals and, similarly, Lestat has not the slightest regard for animal life. The latter is made clear by Lestat's treatment of the field rat he uses to demonstrate to Louis the dietary viability of the rat's blood: he 'took the rat to the wine glass, slashed its throat, and filled the cup rapidly with blood' before then sending the rat 'hurtling over the gallery railing' (33). The vampires in these earlier texts evidently 'subscribe to mainstream Western [and speciesist] ideas about the status of animals—the idea that humans are in an exalted moral category, and ... that animals exist to serve human purposes'. It follows from this that, if vampires must kill, 'it's better to kill a non-human animal' (Kazez 25–26, 27). But this argument cannot be levelled against the Cullens.[8] Not only are they 'protectors of human life' (*Eclipse* 27), they are protectors of the ecosystem too.

Another indication of the Cullens' eco-friendly and sustainable dietary habits is their feeding routine. Unlike Louis' 'nightly killings' (*Interview* 120), the Cullens' consumption of animal blood is less frequent and more moderate. We know this because Bella keeps a close account of the minuscule changes in Edward's eye colour, which records his level of hunger. Immediately after feeding, Edward's eyes are soft butterscotch. When he is starving, his eyes turn black. In the weeks between satiation and starvation, Bella notes the shades in-between: topaz first and 'in two weeks [time] onyx' (*Twilight* 201). There are times when Edward and his family do feed more frequently than strictly necessary, such as when they believe it will be difficult to control their hunger (as Edward does before his first date with Bella) or when they require greater strength to fight other vampires. While such feeding habits suggest that there is an anthropocentric inflection to the Cullens' vegetarianism—they clearly believe it is better to kill another animal than another human—this kind of hunting excursion is

---

[8] Critics like Elizabeth Tenga and Zimmerman disagree (80). See their article.

unusual and occurs only a handful of times in the saga.[9] Further, these events should not be used to dismiss the fact that the Cullens normally go weeks without feeding, taking only what they need. Unlike Claudia, Lestat, and Angelus, they are controlled, moderate, and conscientious, rather than voracious consumers.

This eco-conscious facet of the Cullens' diet is important, for although something like their sense of morality can be found elsewhere in the genre, their concern for the ecosystem is new. If vampires are 'personifications of their age' (Auerbach 1), figures which 'emerge in various historical contexts as mythological manifestations of collective anxieties and desires' (Atkinson 225), we find with the Cullens a vampire suitable for our own age, the Anthropocene.[10] In their care to avoid ecological degradation and not damage the ecosystem by over-hunting, coupled with their efforts to support the wider ecosystem by controlling deer and elk populations, the Cullens model an environmental responsibility attuned to mindful consumption (eating seasonably and judiciously) and conservation. In so doing, they can be said to register some of the very real and pressing concerns of the twenty-first century. This is the inference that Leah Lamb (former founding producer and host of Al Gore's Current TV channel (2005–13), a cable station devoted to environmental issues) draws from her reading of *Twilight*. She writes:

> I think I love this story, because in so many ways … I live this story. Every day, I fight my impulses in the name of saving the planet as we know it. The story of the times we live in is that the nature of our culture and society is to consume past the point of sustainability.

Lamb concludes that 'the earth is our host and we are one helluva mega coven of vampires. If vampires can make conscious decisions to find new alternatives to sucking blood and killing the things they desire, then so can we' (qtd. in McFarland-Taylor 146, 147).

---

[9] With regard to Edward and Bella, the former admits that the more time he spends around Bella, the easier he finds it to resist his desire to feed on her (*Twilight* 245, 262–63, 267). Consequently, Edward's need to feed more regularly, and thus consume more voraciously, diminishes quite quickly after their first date.

[10] Further proof of the saga's eco-awareness can be found in *Fifty Shades of Grey*, E.L James' widely popular erotic novel that began as *Twilight* fanfic. For an ecocritical analysis of *Fifty Shades of Grey*, see Arjomand and McFarland-Taylor 41–67.

Not everyone shares Lamb's view of the novels. As Isla Myers-Smith argues, with their 'mindless and excessive auto acquisition and use' ('Edward's Volvo, the silver S60R, Rosalie's BMW M3, Carlisle's Mercedes S55 AMG, Emmet's Jeep Wrangler, and Alice's Porsche 911 Turbo') and penchant for driving at 'fuel inefficient speeds', the Cullens are 'anything but green-friendly inhabitant types' (qtd. in Mc Elroy and Mc Elroy 85). Their supernatural ability to run at extremely fuel-efficient speeds, which makes cars unnecessary for them, amplifies Myers-Smith's argument. James and Ella Mc Elroy, adding up the ecological cost of the Cullens' vampirism, note that the children 'purchase but never eat generous servings of cafeteria food' and that, as vampires who do not sleep (something else not shared by the other texts considered in this study), the Cullens are 'on the go ... with a breathtaking 24/7 schedule ... wherein more and more lights are used and more and more stuff is required on an *ad infinitum* basis'. According to Mc Elroy and Mc Elroy, these are two more 'no-no[s] when it comes to looking at [the Cullens'] carbon footprint' (85). Other critics argue that the considerable amount of product tie-ins and merchandise generated by the series—'make up', 'condoms', 'soap', underpants', 'tampon cases', diaper covers, cookbooks', 'freezable dildos' and 't-shirts', to name a few (McFarland-Taylor 151)—make the saga, and its eco-friendly vampires, 'the worst ecological catastrophe of the 21st century' (Masland qtd. in McFarland-Taylor 151). Clearly, the Cullens are not perfect; like Adam and Eve (those other vampires of the Anthropocene, as seen in *Only Lovers Left Alive*), the Cullens 'are not ... paragons of eco-conscious living' (Mansbridge 216). Perhaps this only adds to the success of the saga's vegetarian analogy. With their efforts to do some ecological good while maintaining some unsustainable habits (their consumption of white goods like cars, boats, designer clothing and so on), the Cullens reflect the experience of many Western, white, middle-class humans in the Anthropocene (McFarland-Taylor 127). Like us, they have begun to adopt a less extractive existence, and again like us, they have not found the perfect solution. However, in their efforts to find a solution (eating judiciously and so on) and do some environmental good, the Cullens offer a model for its readers to imitate (only in relation to how we eat) and a mirror to our own 'unsustainable habits' (Mansbridge 216).

We may usefully situate in the Anthropocene another often-mentioned aspect of the saga, namely its religious overtone. As Laura Wright points out, Meyer 'presents us with a kind of salvation narrative, one that is completely dependent upon the politics of diet' (56). While this is true—Carlisle does share with Bella his hope that by abstaining from human blood he and his family might have a chance of qualifying for redemption (*New Moon* 36–37)—it is important 'to think beyond the premise', so popular with critics such as Wright, Lori Branch and Marc Shaw, 'that Meyer's brand of fictionalized creature … is somehow the direct outcome of [her] unique Mormon cosmology' (Mc Elroy and Mc Elroy 88).[11] Such readings flatten the broader concerns of the novel. Without dismissing theological readings, I propose that there is another way of understanding the link between the Cullens' diet and their salvation that is not related to their metaphysical status in the afterlife, but rather informed by the novels' ecological concerns (Mc Elroy and Mc Elroy 88).

As I have suggested, the Cullens are the vampires that the twenty-first century needs, who reflect our growing and increasingly urgent environmental concerns. But they do not just reflect our anxieties. They reflect our desire, for want of a better phrase, to save the planet as a whole. Read in this way, the saga's salvation narrative, as it relates to the Cullens' diet, can be seen to function as an allegory for human-earth relations in the Anthropocene. The Cullens' version of a vegetarian diet may be good for their soul (a connection made by Whedon in *Buffy*), but a vegetarian diet in its usual sense as abstention from meat is also good for the planet. In 2018, an Oxford University study found that 'avoiding meat and dairy is the single biggest way to reduce your impact on the Earth' (Carrington). That same year Greenpeace found that

> global meat and dairy production and consumption must be cut in half by 2050 to avoid dangerous climate change and keep the Paris Agreement on track. If left unchecked, agriculture is projected to produce 52% of global greenhouse gas emissions in the coming decades, 70% of which will come from meat and dairy. ('Greenpeace')

To these remarks, some might reply, of course, that the Cullens are not vegetarian—they still drink blood from and thus kill animals. But, as noted in the Introduction, the Cullens are 'vegetarian' in the sense that, like human vegetarians, they draw nourishment from one step further down the chain of being than is conventional for their species, and as this chapter

---

[11] For further discussion of how Meyer's Mormonism influences her saga, see Granger; Schwartzman; Jeffers; and Wilson, *Seduced by Twilight*, chapter six.

has argued, they provide a defamiliarizing echo of our own ecological vegetarianism. And here, within the saga's religious overtone, we find another resonance: a vegetarian diet, in its different inflections, engenders salvation, not only for Meyer's vampires, but for the earth and its many inhabitants (human, plant or animal).

The relevance of the Anthropocene as a historical context for the saga is also evident in its broader depiction of, and engagement with, the natural world. As critics have noted, the saga is deeply attuned to the environment in which it unfolds, 'with its attendant meteorological conditions (wet rains), botanical lushness (damp/dank greeneries), apposite forest clearings (Edward and Bella's Edenic-inclined meadow), and remote beach sites as select border habitats' (Mc Elroy and Mc Elroy 81). This attentiveness is evident from *Twilight*'s opening sentence in which Bella describes Forks as a 'small town [that] exists under a near-constant cover of clouds', where 'it rains ... more than any other place in the United States of America' (3). Her attention to the natural world continues throughout the novel. On the drive home to Forks from the airport, for example, Bella's focus is on the environment around her. 'Everything was green', she tells us, 'the trees, their trunks covered with moss, their branches hanging with a canopy of it, the ground covered with ferns'— even the air 'filtered down greenly through the leaves' (7). Later, we get minute descriptions of the rockpools that line La Push beach that are 'teeming with life' (filled with 'bouquets of brilliant anemones', 'crabs', 'starfish', a 'small black eel with white racing stripes', and 'bright green weeds' [101]); a driftwood fire that burns 'strange blue and green flames' thanks to the saltwater (100); and descriptions of rain from a previous day having 'frozen solid—coating the needles on the trees in fantastic, gorgeous patterns' (45). Such descriptions, as Mc Elroy and Mc Elroy point out, 'promote at the level of rhizome', an inescapable

> sense that the human creature is but one small part of an intricate ecological system and that people should therefore recognize, no matter how belatedly, that, far from being part of a superior species called *homo sapiens*, they are only one finite speciate element in a planetary eco-system which humans depend on for their survival. (87)

Indeed, humans *are* but one species in the saga, which adds werewolves to its multispecies cast of humans, vampires, animal and plant life forms. Meyer's werewolves (the Quileutes) are not 'children of the moon'

(*Breaking Dawn* 704) in the traditional Gothic sense.[12] They do not need a full moon to transform (*New Moon* 312), nor do they 'continue their species by infecting others the way true werewolves do'. Instead, their ability to change into a wolf is 'genetic'—'they have merely inherited this skill from their fathers' (*Breaking Dawn* 705), as Aro explains. While they differ from traditional werewolves in many respects, the Quileutes do share their kind's enmity for vampires, who are considered 'the natural enemies of the wolf' (*Twilight* 107). According to Jacob Black, a Quileute werewolf (who is also Bella's best friend), killing vampires is 'what we're made for' (*New Moon* 311). However, over the course of the saga, this enmity is eased via a series of steps that bring these warring species together—the first of which is the Cullens' animal-blood diet. This step goes back to the first contact between the Quileute werewolves and the Cullens. Instead of hunting the Cullens, as is standard practice, the Quileutes entered into a treaty with them because they 'didn't hunt the way others of their kind did' (*Twilight* 108).[13] Here, a change in diet once again opens the possibility of a change in relations between species, this time between vampire and werewolf rather than vampire and human.

The terms of the treaty are simple: the Cullens can live amongst humans in Forks and without danger from the Quileute wolves so long as they do not bite or turn a human or enter Quileute territory. These conditions do not erase the divide between vampires and werewolves. They seem at first to consolidate them, by locating each species within different portions of the country. But this should not be allowed to eclipse the work that the treaty does in negotiating the overarching species enmity that, if the legend is to be believed, is genetically (and supernaturally) ingrained in both vampires and werewolves. By entering into a treaty with the Cullens, the werewolves enter a new, even if also extremely tenuous, a relationship of cross-species trust and coexistence, which is made possible by the Cullens' animal-blood diet. Here we find, once again, the link between diet and species relations, which is in the saga to negotiate, navigate, and ultimately

---

[12] Several critics have written at length on the saga's problematic admixture of Native Americans with werewolves. See Jensen; Leggatt and Burnett 35–36; Wilson, 'Civilised Vampires' and *Seduced by Twilight* 10, 37–39, 157–78. See also Willus-Chun.

[13] This account is corroborated in *Eclipse*, by Jacob's father, Billy Black, when he describes the Quileutes first contact with Carlisle and, more particularly, this vampire's 'strange yellow eyes [which] gave some proof to his claim that they were not the same as other blood drinkers' (259).

diminish the power of species boundaries.[14] Importantly, this treaty does not extend to broader species enmity: the Quileute werewolves still view vampires who drink human blood as the enemy and join the Cullens in fighting such vampires when they venture into Forks.[15] Thus rather than dividing species, the treaty distinguishes between ways of life, in which quite different species ((vegetarian) vampires and werewolves) can enter into an alliance with each other.

The saga's interest in inter-species relations is also found in Jacob's relationship with Renesmee—Bella's and Edward's half-human, half-vampire, daughter—on whom he imprints (*Breaking Dawn* 359–60). In the saga's fictional world, imprinting is 'one of those bizarre things [that werewolves] have to deal with'. It is like 'love at first sight', Jacob explains, but 'more powerful than that', 'more absolute' (*Eclipse* 122, 123). The rationale behind imprinting is not known for certain, but both Sam Uley, the Quileute werewolves' leader, and Billy Black, Jacob's father, have their own theories. According to Sam, a werewolf imprints on the person with whom *he* has the best reproductive chance to 'pass on the wolf gene' (female wolves cannot procreate).[16] Billy places the emphasis elsewhere: imprinting is designed to make the next generation of wolves 'stronger' (*Breaking Dawn* 318).[17] The union of Renesmee (who is half-human and half-vampire) and Jacob (who is a werewolf), supports the latter. By combining the vampiric traits that Renesmee has (hard skin, supernatural gifts like mind-reading, strength and speed) with Jacob's (strength, speed, accelerated healing), their offspring could draw on the strengths of both species. But, if taken as a metaphor, their union has a more powerful significance: the strongest generation is that which is marked by inter-species

---

[14] The possibility that an animal-blood diet might help resolve some of the tensions between vampires and werewolves is not present in *The Vampire Diaries*, *The Southern Vampire Mysteries* or *True Blood*. In the first, the bite of a werewolf bite is normally fatal to vampires, as seen in the death of Rose ('The Descent'), unless neutralized by Klaus's hybrid blood ('As I Lay Dying'). The third, following the novels, takes this enmity a step further by showing werewolves to be slaves of the vampire king of Mississippi.

[15] For instance, in *Eclipse*, the wolves join the Cullens and fight Victoria and her newborn vampire army (537–53); an alliance they continue in *Breaking Dawn* (682–83) when the Volturi come to destroy Renesmee and the Cullen family.

[16] For a critique of this, see Whitton 128–29.

[17] Natalie Wilson and Anna Silver have read the phenomena of imprinting in less optimistic terms, as racist and sexist respectively. See Wilson, *Seduced by Twilight* 173 and Silver 130, 133. See also Donnelly 188–89.

mixing, which conjures in turn an extremely optimistic and hopeful vision of a multispecies future which includes humans, werewolves and vampires.[18]

However, the union of humans, vampires and werewolves, as seen in relations between Jacob and Renesmee, is not the most radical species exchange found in the saga. That is reserved for Bella and her decision to 'change species allegiance' (Mc Elroy and Mc Elroy 83) and become a vampire. This choice sets Bella apart from the female protagonists in the other works in this study. Sookie, Elena and Buffy may love vampires, but they do not want to become one themselves. Sookie repeatedly makes this point; so too does Elena (who *does* however briefly become a vampire in the third season ('The Departed'), only to be cured of the affliction in a later season ('I'd Leave My Happy Home for You'); and Buffy, unsurprisingly, would rather die than become what she exists to destroy. Only Louis makes the same choice as Bella. Whereas he comes bitterly to regret it—he records his vampiric life history as a warning to anyone who would seek his fate—Bella revels in the change. She is 'quite graceful—even for a vampire' and, unlike Louis, has an unusual control over her bloodlust,[19] which allows her to avoid becoming 'the crazed killing-machine' that other newborn vampires become.[20] Consequently, Bella 'fit[s] right in with the Cullens from [her] first day', as she proudly declares, and is 'a good vampire right away'. All of this leads Bella to proclaim that 'after eighteen years of mediocrity' as a human, 'I had found my true place in the world, the place I fit, the place I shined'—'it was like I had been born to be a vampire' (*Breaking Dawn* 409, 466, 523–24).

This transformation is not always described in positive terms. As critics like to point out, Bella's desire to become a vampire is only realised through Edward's insistence on marriage: he will make her a vampire but mandates that Bella must marry him first. For Anthea Taylor, this is evidence of Edward's desire to have absolute control over Bella (42). Natalie Wilson sees an even darker heteronormative ideal at play in Bella's transformation:

---

[18] Critics like Judith Leggatt and Kristin Burnett disagree and discern 'something more complicated' (43) in their study of Jacob's and Renesmee's union against the backdrop of settler-Quileute politics. See their article.

[19] When Bella, while hunting for the first time, comes across the scent of humans, who are still nearby, she withdraws from the hunt by holding her breath and running in the opposite direction (*Breaking Dawn* 417–19).

[20] See the chapter 'Newborn' (*Eclipse*) for a profile of newborn vampires.

in *Twilight*, the vampire is not killed—rather, the human is. Killing Bella, turning her into a vampire, restores her "proper" sexuality and ensconces her within the good Cullen family. ... Instead of turning her into a more lustful creature, [Bella's change into a vampire] ultimately turns her into a chaste and devoted wife and mother. (*Seduced by Twilight* 22)[21]

These arguments cannot simply be dismissed, but they should neverthe-less not be allowed entirely to eclipse the positive posthumanist power of Bella's transformation. By making the decision to become a vampire, Bella 'subvert[s] the ... idea of ... species purity' traditionally upheld in vampire texts (Nayar 132). (*Buffy* is a good example of this.) Her slide into vampir-ism is, as Pramod Nayar points out, a 'step toward ... posthumanist species cosmopolitanism' (132).

Bella's transformation also brings her closer to the natural world. As Parmiter notes, although Bella may be dead, she is more 'alive to the pulse of the natural world' (229) than ever before. While hunting for the first time, Bella's heightened senses and vampire eyes wakens her to the forest, which now seems 'much more alive that I'd ever known—small creatures whose existence I'd never guessed at teemed in the leaves around me' (*Breaking Dawn* 410). She 'also grows more protective' (Parmiter 229) and 'worries about the forest getting hurt' (*Breaking Dawn* 413). Although the human Bella was deeply appreciative of and attentive to the natural world, the vampire Bella gains 'greater access to and appreciation for everything living', 'from the dust motes in the air ... to the vibrant green of her shady refuge' (Parmiter 228). We can therefore say that, by becoming a vampire, Bella does more than cross the divide between human and vampire (Parmiter 229), she also narrows that gap that, as a human, divided her from nature. Here, as elsewhere in Meyer's saga, 'good' vampires 'seem *more* natural than their human neighbours, in closer contact and balance with the green world' (Parmiter 228).

What then can readers learn from Bella's transformation? As Parmiter points out, 'the difficulty in celebrating Bella's transformation is that none of us can follow her lead; though Bella can get closer to the natural world by joining the ranks of the undead, she hardly presents a model for her readers to emulate' (229). What readers can model instead, is the care with which Bella and her vampiric family engage with the environment, a

---

[21] See also Rocha 274–78; Silver 132; and Williamson 146–50. For an opposing view, see McFarland-Taylor 143–44.

care that extends to other species and to the ecosystem as a whole. They still feed on animals, but they do so in a sustainable fashion. Critics like Simon Bacon may denounce the saga for having 'defanged' the vampire, but it can be argued that in a world under increasing ecological threat, a 'defanged' or vegetarian vampire is the vampire we need (McFarland-Taylor 127)—a truth confirmed by the saga's phenomenal success and equally phenomenal impact on the vampire genre. As Scott Meslow observes, 'Stephenie Meyer hasn't left vampire fiction in the same place she found it'. Anne Rice may have brought animal blood to the genre, but with her saga, Meyer takes that blood and makes it '"green"' (McFarland-Taylor 2, 144). As the next two chapters detail, in Meyer's wake, vampire fiction had adopted a distinctly eco-friendly tone, as the vampires in *The Vampire Diaries* and *True Blood* heed the Cullens' call to explore more sustainable, less destructive ways of living in this more-than-human earth. Like the Cullens, the vampires in these texts also make 'ethical decisions about how [their] food choices affect their environments' (Parmiter 226) and the human and nonhuman actors on this earth.

Works Cited

Ames, Melissa. 'Twilight Follows Tradition: Anaylzing "Biting" Critiques of Vampire Narratives for Their Portrayals of Gender and Sexuality.' Click et al., pp. 37–54.

Anatol, Giselle Liza, editor. *Bringing Light to Twilight: Perspectives on the Pop Culture Phenomenon*. Palgrave Macmillan, 2011.

Atkinson, Ted. '"Blood Petroleum": *True Blood*, the BP Oil Spill, and Fictions of Energy/Culture.' *Journal of American Studies*, vol. 47, no. 1, Feb. 2013, pp. 213–29. *JSTOR*, www.jstor.org/stable/23352514.

Averill, Lindsey. 'Un-biting the Apple and Killing the Womb: Genesis, Gender, and Gynocide.' Parke and Wilson, pp. 224–37.

Bacon, Simon. 'Eat Me! The Morality of Hunger in Vampiric Cuisine.' *Images of the Modern Vampire: The Hip and the Atavistic*, edited by Barbara Brodman and James E. Doan, Farleigh Dickinson UP, 2013, pp. 41–51. *ProQuest Ebook Central*, ebookcentral.proquest.com/lib/unimelb/detail.action?docID=1466965.

Bealer, Tracy L. 'Of Monsters and Man: Toxic Masculinity and the Twenty-First Century Vampire in the *Twilight* Saga.' Anatol, pp. 139–52.

Branch, Lori. 'Carlisle's Cross: Locating the Post-Secular Gothic.' Clarke and Osborne, pp. 60–79.

Buttsworth, Sara. 'CinderBella: Twilight, Fairy Tales, and the Twenty-First Century American Dream.' Reagin, pp. 47–69.

Carrington, Damian. 'Avoiding Meat and Dairy Is "Single Biggest Way" to Reduce Your Impact on Earth.' *The Guardian*, 1 Jun. 2018, www.theguardian.com/environment/2018/may/31/avoiding-meat-and-dairy-is-single-biggest-way-to-reduce-your-impact-on-earth. Accessed 16 June 2018.

Clarke, Amy M., and Marijane Osborn, editors. *The Twilight Mystique: Critical Essays on the Novels and Films*. McFarland, 2010.

Clayton, Wickham, and Sarah Harman, editors. *Screening Twilight: Critical Approaches to a Cinematic Phenomenon*. I.B. Tauris, 2014.

Click, Melissa, et al., editors. *Bitten by Twilight: Youth Culture, Media, and the Vampire Franchise*. Peter Lang Publishing, 2010.

Donnelly, Ashley. 'Denial and Salvation: The *Twilight* Saga and Heteronormative Patriarchy.' Parke and Wilson, pp. 178–93.

Frank, Alexandra C. 'All-Consuming Passions: Vampire Foodways in Contemporary Film and Television.' *What's Eating You? Food and Horror on Screen*, edited by Cynthia J. Miller et al., Bloomsbury Academic, 2017, pp. 339–52.

George, Sam, and Bill Hughes, editors. *Open Graves, Open Minds: Representations of the Vampire and the Undead from the Enlightenment to the Present Day*, Manchester UP, 2013. *JSTOR*, www.jstor.org/stable/j.ctt18mvm36.

Gerhards, Lea. 'Vampires "On a Special Diet": Identity and the Body in Contemporary Media Texts.' *Dracula and the Gothic in Literature, Pop Culture and the Arts*, edited by Isabel Ermida, Brill, 2015, pp. 237–58. *ProQuest Ebook Central*, ebookcentral.proquest.com/lib/unimelb/detail.action?docID= 4007474.

Granger, John. 'Mormon Vampires in the Garden of Eden: What the Bestselling Twilight Series Has in Store for Young Readers.' *Touchstone*, Nov/ Dec. 2009, www.touchstonemag.com/archives/article.php?id=22-08-024-f. Accessed 29 Sept. 2018.

'Greenpeace Calls For Decrease in Meat and Dairy Production and Consumption For a Healthier Planet.' *Greenpeace International*, 5 Mar. 2018, www.greenpeace.org/international/press-release/15111/greenpeace-calls-for-decrease-in-meat-and-dairy-production-and-consumption-for-a-healthier-planet/. Accessed 16 June 2018.

Harris, Charlaine. *All Together Dead*. 2007. Gollancz, 2009.

Housel, Rebecca, and J. Jeremy Wisnewski, editors. *Twilight and Philosophy: Vampires, Vegetarians, and the Pursuit of Immortality*. John Wiley and Sons, 2009.

Jeffers, Susan. 'Bella and the Choice Made in Eden.' Clarke and Osborn, pp. 137–51.

Jensen, Kristian. 'Noble Werewolves or Native Shape-Shifters?' Clarke and Osborn, pp. 92–106.

Kane, Kathryn. 'A Very Queer Refusal: The Chilling Effect of the Cullens' Heteronormative Embrace.' Click et al., pp. 103–18.

Kazez, Jean. '"Dying to Eat": The Vegetarian Ethics of *Twilight*.' Housel and Wisnewski, pp. 25–28.

Klonsky, David E., et al., editors. *The Psychology of Twilight*. BenBella Books, Inc, 2011.

Larsson, Mariah, and Ann Steiner, editors. *Interdisciplinary Approaches to Twilight: Studies in Fiction, Media and a Contemporary Cultural Experience*. Nordic Academic Press, 2012. *ProQuest Ebook Central*, ebookcentral.proquest.com/lib/unimelb/detail.action?docID=940046.

Leavenworth, Maria Lindgren, and Malin Isaksson. *Fanged Fan Fiction: Variations on Twilight, True Blood and the Vampire Diaries*. McFarland, 2013. *ProQuest Ebook Central*, ebookcentral.proquest.com/lib/unimelb/detail.action?docID=1286896.

Leggatt, Judith, and Kristin Burnett. 'Biting Bella: Treaty Negotiation, Quileute History, and Why "Team Jacob" is Doomed to Lose.' Reagin, pp. 26–46.

Liedl, Jandice. 'Carlisle Cullen and the Witch Hunts of Puritan London.' Reagin, pp. 145–62.

Magnusson, Gert. 'Are Vampires Evil? Categorizations of Vampires, and Angelus and Spike as the Immoral and the Amoral.' *Slayage: The International Journal of Buffy+*, vol. 9, no. 2, fall 2012, www.whedonstudies.tv/uploads/2/6/2/8/26288593/magnusson_2__slayage_9.2.pdf.

Mansbridge, Joanna. 'Endangered Vampires of the Anthropocene: Jim Jarmusch's *Only Lovers Left Alive* and the Ecology of Romance.' *Genre: Forms of Discourse and Culture*, vol. 53, no. 2, Dec. 2019, pp. 207–28. *Duke UP*, https://doi-org.eu1.proxy.openathens.net/10.1215/00166928-7965805.

Mc Elroy, James, and Emma Catherine Mc Elroy. 'Eco-Gothics for the Twenty-First Century.' Clarke and Osborn, pp. 80–91.

McFarland-Taylor, Sarah. *Ecopiety: Green Media and the Dilemma of Environmental Virtue*. NYU Press, 2019.

McMahon, Jennifer L. '*Twilight* of an Idol: Our Fatal Attraction to Vampires.' Housel and Wisnewski, pp. 193–208.

Meslow, Scott. 'After "Twilight": Where Do Vampires in Pop Culture Go from Here?' *The Atlantic*, 19 Nov. 2012, www.theatlantic.com/entertainment/archive/2012/11/after-twilight-where-do-vampires-in-pop-culture-go-from-here/265393/. Accessed 29 Sept. 2018.

Meyer, Stephenie. *Breaking Dawn*. Atom, 2008.

———. *Eclipse*. Little, Brown, 2007.

———. *Midnight Sun*. Atom, 2020.

———. *New Moon*. Little, Brown, 2006.

———. *Twilight*. Little, Brown, 2005.

Miller, Melissa. 'Maybe Edward Is the Most Dangerous Thing Out There: The Role of Patriarchy.' Parke and Wilson, pp. 165–77.

Nayar, Pramod K. *Posthumanism*. Polity, 2014.

Nicol, Rhonda. '"When You Kiss Me, I Want To Die": Arrested Feminism in *Buffy the Vampire Slayer* and The *Twilight* Series.' Anatol, pp. 113–23.

Ní Fhlainn, Sorcha. *Postmodern Vampires: Film, Fiction, and Popular Culture.* Palgrave Macmillan, 2019. *Springer Link,* https://doi.org/10.1057/978-1-137-58377-2.

Nuxi. 'Anti-Feminism: Bella Swan and the Illusion of Choice.' *Fanpop,* www.fanpop.com/clubs/critical-analysis-of-twilight/articles/29723/title/anti-feminism-bella-swan-illusion-choice. Accessed 28 July 2018.

Parke, Maggie, and Natalie Wilson, editors. *Theorizing Twilight: Critical Essays on What's at Stake in a Post-Vampire World.* McFarland, 2011. *ProQuest Ebook Central,* ebookcentral.proquest.com/lib/unimelb/detail.action?docID=773281.

Parmiter, Tara K. 'Green is the New Black: Ecophobia and the Gothic Landscape in the *Twilight* Series.' Anatol, pp. 221–33.

Piatti-Farnell, Lorna. *The Vampire in Contemporary Popular Literature.* Routledge, 2014.

Preece, Rod. *Sins of the Flesh: A History of Vegetarian Thought.* UBC Press, 2008. *ProQuest Ebook Central,* ebookcentral.proquest.com/lib/unimelb/detail.action?docID=3412608.

Reagin, Nancy R., editor. *Twilight and History.* John Wiley and Sons, Inc., 2010.

Rice, Anne. *Interview with the Vampire.* 1976. Sphere, 2008.

Rocha, Lauren. 'Wife, Mother, Vampire: The Female Role in the Twilight Series.' *Journal of International Women's Studies,* vol. 15, no. 2, July 2014, pp. 267–79. *ProQuest,* www.proquest.com/docview/1553397506/3F819888D15D421F PQ/17?accountid=12372.

Rosenberg, Robin S. 'Vegetarian Vamps: On Changing Hard-to-Change Habits.' Klonsky et al., pp. 115–32.

Schwartzman, Sarah. 'Is *Twilight* Mormon?' Clarke and Osborn, pp. 121–36.

Seifert, Christine. 'Bite Me! (Or Don't).' *Bitch Media: Feminist Response to Pop Culture,* no. 42, winter, 2009, pp. 23–25, www.bitchmedia.org/article/bite-me-or-dont. Accessed 24 July 2019.

Shaw, Marc E. 'For the Strength of Bella? Meyer, Vampires, and Mormonism.' Housel and Wisnewski, pp. 227–31.

Silver, Anna. '*Twilight* is Not Good for Maidens: Gender, Sexuality, and the Family in Stephenie Meyer's *Twilight* Series.' *Studies in the Novel,* vol. 42, no. 1 and 2, 2010, pp. 121–38.

Smith, Michelle J. 'The Postmodern Vampire in "Post-race" America: HBO's *True Blood.*' George and Hughes, pp. 192–209.

Spooner, Catherine. 'Gothic Charm School; or, How Vampires Learned to Sparkle.' George and Hughes, pp. 146–64.

Taylor, Anthea. 'The Urge Towards Love Is an Urge Towards (Un)death: Romance, Masochistic Desire and Postfeminism in the *Twilight* Novels.' *International Journal of Cultural Studies,* vol. 15, no. 1, 2012, pp. 31–46. *Sage Journals,* https://doi.org/10.1177/1367877911399204.

Torkelson, Anne. 'Violence, Agency, and the Women of *Twilight*.' Parke and Wilson, pp. 209–23.

Toscano, Margaret. 'Mormon Mortality and Immortality in Stephenie Meyer's Twilight Series.' Click et al., pp. 21–33.

Whitton, Merrine. '"One Is Not Born a Vampire but Becomes One": Motherhood and Masochism in *Twilight*.' Anatol, pp. 125–37.

Williamson, Milly. 'Let Them All in: The Evolution of the "Sympathetic" Vampire.' *Screening the Undead: Vampires and Zombies in Film and Television*, edited by Leon Hunt and Sharon Lockyer, I.B. Tauris, 2013, pp. 137–71. *ProQuest Ebook Central*, ebookcentral.proquest.com/lib/unimelb/detail.action?docID=1686629.

Willus-Chun, Cynthia. 'Touring the Twilight Zone: Cultural Tourism and Commodification on the Olympic Peninsula.' Click et al., pp. 261–80.

Wilson, Natalie. 'Civilized Vampires Versus Savage Werewolves: Race and Ethnicity in the Twilight Series.' Click et al., pp. 55–70.

———. *Seduced by Twilight: The Allure and Contradictory Messages of the Popular Saga*. McFarland, 2011. *ProQuest Ebook Central*, ebookcentral.proquest.com/lib/unimelb/detail.action?docID=679329.

Wright, Laura. *The Vegan Studies Project: Food, Animals, and Gender in the Age of Terror*. Georgia UP, 2015. *JSTOR*, www.jstor.org/stable/j.ctt183q3vb.

TV

'As I Lay Dying.' Directed by John Behring. *The Vampire Diaries*, season 2, episode 22, The CW, 12 May 2011. *Stan*, https://www.stan.com.au/.

'Damage.' Directed by Jefferson Kibbee. *Angel*, season 5, episode 11, Mutant Enemy, 2003. *Disney Plus*, https://www.disneyplus.com/.

'The Departed.' Directed by John Behring. *The Vampire Diaries*, season 3, episode 22, The CW, 10 May 2012. *Stan*, https://www.stan.com.au/.

'The Descent.' Directed by Marcos Siega. *The Vampire Diaries*, season 2, episode 12, The CW, 27 Jan. 2011. *Stan*, https://www.stan.com.au/.

'The Dinner Party.' Directed by Marcos Siega. *The Vampire Diaries*, season 2, episode 15, The CW, 17 Feb. 2011. *Stan*, https://www.stan.com.au/.

'I'd Leave My Happy Home for You.' Directed by Jesse Warn. *The Vampire Diaries*, season 6, episode 20, The CW, 30 Apr. 2015. *Stan*, https://www.stan.com.au/.

'Something Blue'. Directed by Nick Marck. *Buffy the Vampire Slayer*, season 4, episode 9, The WB, 30 Nov. 1999. *Stan*, https://www.stan.com.au/.

CHAPTER 5

Banked Blood and Bunnies: Ethical Predation in *The Vampire Diaries*

Abstract This chapter places the long-running television series *The Vampire Diaries* in dialogue with the book series on which it is based, written by L.J. Smith. As this chapter demonstrates, in its depiction of vampiric diets, the television deviates substantially from its source material. Here, strict attention is paid to the historical contexts in which each appeared. The first half of the chapter examines some of the features of L.J. Smith's novels (the romance plot, its depiction of Stefan's animal-blood diet) and the genre to which they belong. The second half of the chapter discusses the television series. Of particular importance here is the television series' addition of donated human blood, drawn from hospital blood, to the vampire's menu and the emphasis placed on Stefan's animal-blood diet, which moves to the centre of the narrative. These deviations make visible the Anthropocene as a compelling context for thinking about shifts in the vampire's appetites and feeding patterns/preferences.

Keywords *The Vampire Diaries* • Animal-blood diet • Donated human blood • Banked blood • Blood bags

As argued in the previous chapter, the recent shift in vampire texts from a human to an animal-blood diet is best understood as a response to the Anthropocene. Extending this argument, this chapter places The CW's

S. Dungan, *Reading the Vegetarian Vampire*, Palgrave Gothic, https://doi.org/10.1007/978-3-031-18350-8_5

long-running television series *The Vampire Diaries* (2009–17) in dialogue with L.J. Smith's early 1990s books on which the television series is based.

This chapter focuses on the changes made in the television series to the story told in the novels, particularly about the vampire's animal-blood diet.[1] In the novels, the animal-blood diet works to foreground the morality of the sympathetic vampire. Contrariwise, in the television series the vampire's animal-blood diet is constellated in new ways, enabling the series to explore the contemporary concerns of the vegetarian vampire. It is this shift from the sympathetic to the vegetarian vampire, as seen in the changes made in the television series to the story told in the novels, that this chapter explores. It argues that these changes register the influence of *Twilight* and the growing popularity of vegetarian vampires in other contemporary vampire texts. Of particular interest is the addition to the vampires' diet in the television series of donated human blood drawn from blood banks, which gives vampires who choose to drink human blood access to more sustainable sources of human blood, while also offering a salient example of ways in which the genre has developed in response not just to *Twilight* but, at least in part, to the Anthropocene.[2]

---

[1] Although a comprehensive discussion of these differences lies outside the scope of this chapter, it is worth noting that the television makes several other (substantial) revisions to Smith's narrative. The witch Bonnie Bennett, for instance, is African American (in the books she is Irish American), and her ancestors are Salem witches, not Irish druids. The Salvatore brothers are also Americanised, depicted as born and raised in Mystic Falls rather than in Renaissance Italy as they are in the novels. In the television series, Damon is even described as having fought for the Confederate Army. To the best of my knowledge, only Ebony Elizabeth Thomas has engaged critically with the change in Bonnie's ethnicity and ancestry (107–42); however, Kimberly McMahon-Coleman and Roslyn Weaver, Janani Subramanian and Jorie Lagerwey have also turned some attention to the identity politics explicit in the television series' decision to depict witches as African American (McMahon-Coleman and Weaver 110; Subramanian and Lagerwey 195), which demands further analysis. The television series' depiction of African Americans, and the series' treatment of Bonnie (as a character and black woman) is also a source of tension online and in fan forums. See, for example, Carter; Jeanna; Lewis; and Thomas 130–34. The absence of African Americans in L.J. Smith's novels is another source of tension online and in fan forums. See, for example, Nuñez. For a particularly thorough discussion of the brother's Americanisation, see McMahon-Coleman 211–24. For an overview of the narrative differences between the novels and the television series, see Crawford 261–70.

[2] Critics have interpreted the consumption of human and animal blood by vampires in the television series as an analogy for drug addiction. See McFarland-Taylor 152–55; McMahon-Coleman 211, 214; McMahon-Coleman and Weaver 140, 155–57; and Frank 344. For a contrasting view, see Leavenworth and Isaksson 165–67.

Before proceeding further, a prefatory note on the novels is required. For the purposes of this chapter, my discussion focuses on the first four novels in the series, on which the television series is based: *The Awakening* (1991), *The Struggle* (1991), *The Fury* (1992) and *Dark Reunion* (1993). Three trilogies, each comprised of three novels, were later added to the series: *The Return* trilogy (*Nightfall* [2009], *Shadow Souls* [2010], *Midnight* [2011]); *The Hunters* trilogy (*Phantom* [2011], *Moonsong* [2012], *Destiny Rising* [2012]); and finally, *The Salvation* trilogy (*Unseen* [2013], *Unspoken* [2013], *Unmasked* [2014]). However, these novels have no impact on the television series' narrative[3] and so, for this reason, can be left safely outside the purview of this chapter.

THE EARLY 1990S: L.J. SMITH
AND THE SYMPATHETIC TRADITION

To illustrate how diet in the television series deviates from the novels, it is first necessary to sketch some of the features of the early 1990s novels and the genre to which they belong. The novels (like the television series) are focused on the relationships between the vampire brothers, Stefan and Damon Salvatore, and Elena Gilbert, the human-turned-vampire with whom they are both in love. As Dudek notes, 'the love they both feel for Elena, and the way [she] feels about them' (41), structures the novels which centres on the brothers' competition for Elena. More is made of this competition in the television series than in the novels: the former 'keep[s] both Stefan and Damon as possible romantic partners for Elena' (Crawford 268), while in the latter Elena only seriously considers Stefan as a plausible partner. The novels also detail (as does the television series) Stefan's and Damon's previous relationship with Katherine von Schwartz (known to the brothers as Katherine Pierce, then as Petrova in the television series), a vampire with whom they were once both in love and who bears an uncanny resemblance to Elena (Crawford 262).[4] Their history

---

[3] For a discussion of these later novels and their relationship to the television series, see Bridgeman.

[4] In the novels, Elena's resemblance to Katherine is treated as something akin to fate. The television series, however, expansively develops this similarity in line with the series' gothic tone and fashions Elena as a doppelganger to Katherine. In season 5, it is revealed that Stefan too is a doppelganger. See McMahon-Coleman 217–20 for more on this topic.

with Katherine, and her appearance in *The Struggle*, provides another source of romantic tension in the novels.

Stefan is also a vegetarian vampire, who chooses to subsist on a diet of animal blood drawn from woodland creatures (rabbits, deer, foxes and so on). Not only does this diet position him as the 'good' brother and therefore a more suitable romantic choice for Elena, as opposed to Damon's 'bad' human-blood drinking, it also enables him to become a part of human society: he attends the local high school, resides in the local boarding house, befriends a handful of his schoolmates (Matt, Bonnie and Meredith) and 'devotes himself to defending the town' (Crawford 97) of Fells Church where the novels are set, first from Katherine and then Klaus, the original vampire from whom all vampires are descended. At first sight, these developments signify the morality of the vegetarian vampire and, more broadly, that the novels situate a change in diet at the heart of what it means to live ethically with other species. However, as I will argue in this section, this is not the case. Although there are elements of what will later become the vegetarian vampire present in the novels—such as Stefan's ability to live alongside, love and desire to protect humans, which will be developed and reworked in the television series—they are constelled in ways that evoke the sympathetic rather than the vegetarian vampire.

That we are dealing in the novels with sympathetic rather than vegetarian vampires owes, in part, to the primary interest of this series, which is the love relationship between Stefan and Elena, and also, again in part, to the historical context in which the series was published. Regarding the former, in the novels, blood-sharing between partners is coded as a love transaction, which Stefan and Elena engage in. This renders his vegetarianism incidental. At the conclusion of the second book, Elena dies and becomes a vampire, which forecloses the possibility of further exploring romantic inter-species relations. Consequently, the novels end up exploring the same sorts of relationships as *Interview*: vampire-vampire relations, as opposed to human-vampire relations centred on Stefan and Elena.

With regard to context, the novels' focus on the sympathetic rather than vegetarian vampire owes something to the influence of *Twilight* and a growing sense of the dangers posed by the Anthropocene. As noted in Chap. 4, after the publication of *Twilight*, the ways in which the vampire's animal-blood diet and human-vampire relations are constelled take new forms that emerge in response to increasingly urgent demands for environmental conservation, sustainability and greater ethical responsibility and care for other species. Lacking both of these contexts and despite some incidental similarities, such as the novels' interest in inter-species relations and diet, Stefan's animal-blood diet, as it appears in the novels, leads to the sympathetic vampire as a love interest. This still speaks to a growing interest in inter-species (human-vampire) relationships, but in this case those relations are used primarily to build sympathy for the vampire, through an understanding of his psychological and emotional complexity. It is not a relationship that explores the kinds of relationships between species needed in the Anthropocene.

These last points are confirmed by the description of Stefan's animal-blood diet in the novels. Although he has chosen to feed on animal and not human blood, the novels (like *Interview*) do not fully develop a dietary ethic in which this choice can be placed. In the first novel, for instance, the only reference to his diet comes when he recounts his early years as a vampire: 'I was living beyond the city gates then', he says, 'half starved, preying on animals, an animal myself' (*The Awakening* 230). In the following novel, Stefan adds only marginally to this account, disclosing that his lifestyle is the result of a vow 'made many centuries ago' to 'not to kill' 'the weak, blundering, but still-human creatures around him' (*The Struggle* 486–87).

David Punter's remarks on *Interview*, quoted earlier, are relevant also to the novels: 'there is a sense, in which [Smith] shirks the questions which lie behind [Stefan's] condition' (161). As in *Interview*, the questions raised by Stefan's diet are answered by turning to the morality of the sympathetic vampire. When Stefan remarks that 'I was ... preying on animals, an animal myself' (*The Awakening* 230), he speaks of himself as an aberration (Leavenworth and Isaksson 162)—a view typical of a sympathetic vampire. Likewise, his recognition that humans are 'weak', 'blundering', but nonetheless 'still-human' (*The Struggle* 486) and thus should not be fed on, suggests a level of sentience that is again typical of the sympathetic vampire and their growing sense of 'virtue' and 'innocence' (Williamson, *Lure* 43), which in turn implies a degree of increasing moral or ethical engagement with human beings.

However, as in *Interview*, any greater ethical or moral engagement with humans is limited at best because, unlike the vegetarian vampire, the sympathetic vampire is driven by self-loathing rather than care for others. They are creatures 'at odds' with their 'vampiric body and the urges [(chiefly bloodlust)] that this body generates' (Williamson, 'Television' par. 2). Like Louis before him, Stefan's struggle against his 'susceptibility to desire and reduction to the drive' (Punter 162) is foregrounded in the novels. In *The Awakening*, for example, he shares his conviction that he is 'a killer ... Evil. A creature born in the dark, destined to live and hunt and hide there forever' (206). Given this condition, he comes to the same conclusion as Louis: to 'find peace was impossible ... because he was evil. He could not change that' (36–37). Again like Louis, Stefan's self-loathing is most pronounced after he feeds (Gerhards 240): after he kills a rabbit, his face 'twist[s] in regret' because 'he hadn't meant to kill it' (*The Awakening* 10); and when Elena recalls finding Stefan feeding on doves, she does not remember his body 'twisted into a bestial crouch', the 'snarl of animal fury on his face', or his blood 'smeared' mouth (208), but 'the sadness in his eyes. Those eyes that had burned like green ice were now dark and empty, hopeless ... there was self-hatred mixed with the sorrow, and bitter condemnation' (210–11). In these instances, we find ample evidence of how, in the novels, diet is used primarily to reveal the sympathetic rather than the vegetarian vampire. It works to foreground Stefan's existential pathos, intensified by his inability to control his hunger, and in so doing garners sympathy, the emotion roused by the sympathetic vampire (Williamson, *Lure* 42).

The predicament of the sympathetic vampire can also be seen in Stefan's surprisingly regular—for a vampire who claims to subsist only on animal blood—diet of human blood. For example, in *The Awakening,* he attacks a homeless man whom he leaves 'half dead' (77), and later, in *The Struggle*, he feeds on the school's football team to regain the strength necessary to fight Damon. In the novels, as in the television series, a diet of animal blood severely weakens a vampire's physical strength and magical powers.[5] In this episode, feeding on human blood is enjoyable rather than merely perfunctory for Stefan: he relishes in it, taking more blood than needed, so that by the time he has fed, he is 'bursting with blood, like an overfed tick' (488). Where the earlier episode illustrates his struggle to abstain from human blood (like Barnabas and Louis, Stefan 'cannot conquer' 'his urges' for human blood, no matter how he might struggle [Day 38]), the latter reveals his tenuous (at best) interest in fostering greater ethical-moral relationships with human beings at large.

---

[5] As Stefan explains to Elena in *The Awakening*, vampires can 'feel minds ... sense their presence and sometimes the nature of their thoughts. We can cast confusion about weaker minds, either to overwhelm them or to bend them to our will ... [and] with enough human blood we can change our shapes [and] become animals'. The more blood consumed, 'the stronger all the Powers become' (230).

Stefan also feeds regularly on Elena, who becomes his main source of sustenance. As noted earlier, that he does so is owing to the role given to blood-sharing between partners. In these novels, blood-sharing 'means love' (*Dark Reunion* 423), which Elena wants for her and Stefan (*The Awakening* 235). Blood-sharing also means sex, as is suggested when he first bites Elena and the pain she initially feels is 'replaced by a feeling of pleasure that made her tremble' (*The Awakening* 238). All this makes clear that his vegetarianism is incidental to the main interests of the story, while also foreclosing the possibility of exploring inter-species relations at any length. It also highlights the novels' lack of interest in exploring the possibilities open by a diet of animal blood. None of this means, of course, that the role of animal blood in these novels can be dismissed. On the contrary, it is an important development, which signals Smith's interest in expanding the romantic potential of the sympathetic vampire.[6] Indeed, the novels realise what is only glimpsed in *Interview*: on the one hand, the vampire's ability to love humans, to feel something other than hunger for them, and, on the other hand, for a human (Elena) to in turn be capable of loving a vampire.[7] Thus, while Stefan's diet of animal blood does not represent the emergence of the vegetarian vampire, it does develop the sympathetic vampire created by Rice, enabling new kinds of relations between humans and vampires to become imaginable. In so doing, the novels open, at the very least, the possibility of a less binary relationship between humans and vampires, which in turn opens the door for a broader acceptance of vampires, as simply another species. These possibilities are foregrounded in the television series through the addition of banked blood to the menu of foods from which its vampires choose.

'TWILIGHT FOR TV': THE VAMPIRE DIARIES AND THE 2000S

The first episode of *The Vampire Diaries* premiered in September 2009, 20 years after the first novel in Smith's series was published. During these decades, *Buffy* had gained cult status; the *Twilight* saga had concluded and made its first foray into the cinema, with *Twilight* (2008); 9 of the 13

---

[6] The same point is made by Joseph Crawford in his analysis of the vampire's emergence as a love interest for humans, writing that 'it was Stefan ... who [through his relationship with Elena] indicated the [romantic] shape [of the genre] to come' (100).

[7] The vampires in *The Southern Vampire Mysteries* and *True Blood* drink from willing human partners but only in the course of intercourse or when severely injured. Blood-sharing in general is not equivalent to love.

novels in *The Southern Vampire Mysteries* had been published; and the first season of *True Blood* had aired to critical acclaim.[8] Thus, by the time the television series' pilot went to air, there was a well-established and widely popular notion of who and what the vegetarian vampire was, one that was largely inconsistent with the vampires featured in Smith's novels. As I will argue in the following pages, the adjustments that the television series makes to the story told in the novels, particularly about Stefan's diet, reflects the television series' contemporary context. Further, as I will show, diet moves to the centre of the television series' narrative, where it does much more than enable the romantic entanglements of the sympathetic vampire.

We can begin to register the influence of *Buffy*, *Twilight*, *The Southern Vampire Mysteries* and *True Blood*, along with the television series' tendency to capitalise on the pop cultural zeitgeist of its time, through the substantial changes made in the television series to Stefan's diet. Firstly, in the television series Stefan adheres (for the most part) to a strict diet of animal blood, using alcohol to help curb his cravings for human blood (McMahon-Coleman and Weaver 157). Unlike in the novels, he is never compelled to feed on humans (although he is compelled to feed on banked blood), nor does he consider reverting to a diet of human blood to regain his strength. Secondly, his decision to subsist on animal blood is shown to be a deliberate moral choice, a point made clear when he discovers that Damon is dating (and feeding on) Elena's best friend, Caroline Forbes. This leads Stefan to implore Damon to leave Caroline alone, telling him that 'they are people Damon. She's not a puppet, she doesn't exist for your amusement. For you to feed on whenever you want to' ('Friday Night Bites' 00:24:38–45). Damon, for whom humans are still food, disagrees, stating 'sure they do. They all do' (00:24:45–51).

Stefan is also committed to protecting human life and works to persuade newly created vampires to adopt his vegetarian lifestyle, first Vicki ('Haunted') and then Caroline ('Bad Moon Rising'). Such efforts increase

---

[8] Initial reviews of the television series were highly aware of its place in an already heavily populated genre and made a frequent comment to the series' relationship to *Twilight* and *True Blood*. See Bianco; Rodman; and Toff. The television series' cast and crew were also frequently asked to comment on comparisons that were being drawn between *The Vampire Diaries*, *Twilight* and *True Blood*. See 'Love Hurts' and 'Kevin Williamson talks about the future of "The Vampire Diaries."' Even Peter Facinelli, the actor who played Carlisle Cullen in the *Twilight* films, commented on the relation between *Twilight* and *The Vampire Diaries* (Sollosi).

the importance and visibility of animal blood in the television series. Vicki ignores Stefan's advice and instead heeds Damon's encouragement to feed on humans, as vampires are meant to do. In contrast, Caroline is convinced by Stefan. Although she treats killing animals flippantly at first, 'isn't killing cute defenceless animals the first step in becoming a serial killer' ('Bad Moon Rising' 00:14:53–57), she quips, she sticks to his vegetarian diet, which earns her the status of a good vampire.

The television series' efforts to foreground matters of diet can also be registered in representations of Stefan as a ripper. As noted in Chap. 4, in the television series' mythos, a ripper is a type of vampire ruled by their bloodlust. Unlike most vampires in the television and novels, who can (and do) practise moderation, once Stefan tastes human blood, he cannot stop ('Miss Mystic Falls'). Instead, as Damon explains to vampire-hunter-turned-ally Alaric Saltzman, Stefan 'feeds so hard he blacks out and rips [his victims] apart' ('The Birthday' 00:13:29–31). His identification as a ripper is important for two reasons. First, his inability to control his blood-lust marks a drastic departure from his portrayal in the novels, where, although he indulges in human blood, he can stop at will. It is also a drastic departure from *Interview* and *Twilight* but not *Buffy*, wherein a vampire's bloodlust is presented as being within the 'realms of free choice or personal control' (McMahon-Coleman 214). This change focuses attention on Stefan's diet (his hunger and lust for blood), which forms the subject of one of the series' central plot lines. When Stefan *does* feed on human blood, he turns into a bloodthirsty monster who has neither care nor compassion for human life.[9] Second, it provides a complementary explanation for why Stefan feeds on animal blood. As he tells Vicki, 'we choose our own path. Our values and our actions, they define who we are' ('Haunted' 00:05:06–12). His diet of animal blood is not just linked to an ethical and moral consideration for human life but figured as a means of deciding the type of vampire he wants to be, the answer to which is ultimately not constrained by his primary urges.

The television series also revises the novels' description of blood-sharing between humans and vampires to better reflect the leading features of contemporary vampire texts, which as I have noted emerged in part through the influence of *Twilight* and in part as a response to the Anthropocene. In the television series, love relationships between humans

---

[9] See, for example, the season one episodes 'Under Control' and 'Miss Mystic Falls', and season three as well, in which he subsists entirely on human blood.

and vampires do not involve transfers of blood. Stefan, for example, never feeds on Elena, not even in the midst of his ripping sprees, during which he is 'shown as desiring to attack other people' (Brennan 6) or when compelled by Klaus to do so ('The Reckoning').[10] When Caroline, after losing control and feeding on Matt, her human boyfriend, tells him 'that she is not "safe"' (Nicol 149), she ends their relationship for fear of hurting him further ('Bad Moon Rising'). Here we find an inversion of the human-vampire relationships seen in the novels, as seen in relations between vampires and humans that, although indirectly, seem to refract notions of greater ethical care and responsibility for other species in response to the Anthropocene. Unsurprisingly, the same can be said for blood and sex in the television series. The two terms are conflated only by vampires like Damon, who views human women as 'plaything[s]' and has no respect for human life ('Klaus' 00:35:51–52).[11] With these key revisions, which align Stefan's abstinence with his morality and separate love from blood-sharing, the television series is able to explore a vampire, the vegetarian vampire, better suited to its time.

The television series does not just update or revise elements of the novels for the twenty-first century, it adds to them. The most important of these is human blood contained by hospital blood bags (donated blood), which adds to the menu of liquids available for its vampires. The addition of donated human blood to the foods able to be chosen by vampires highlights the importance of diet in the television series and shows the television series' efforts to reshape the story told in the novels to more closely accord with the genre's contemporary preoccupations. Drawn from the town's local hospital, donated human blood is the main source of blood (although this was, of course, once taken directly from humans). Over the television series' eight seasons, a variety of vampires subsist on donated blood. Some like Lexi, Anna, Pearl and Henry, choose to drink donated blood out of a respect for, and a desire to live amongst, humans. Others, like the tomb vampires (as they are called), who feel no moral concerns for human life, do so in order to keep a low profile (a strategy that recalls those adopted by travelling vampires in *Interview*) and to avoid detection

[10] Unlike in the novels, in which older vampires can compel younger vampires, in the television series, only original vampires can compel other vampires.

[11] Tellingly, Damon never bites Elena, whom he admits he loves in the second season episode 'Rose'—not even when they briefly become involved in the third season, when she is still human.

by the town's Founder's Council who, besides organising the various Founder's day events and parties, 'do things like round up all the vampires in town and set them on fire in a church' (Houston 271).[12] Although in the television series a diet of animal blood is still represented as the preferable, more ethical choice (Caroline is the paragon of self-control and virtue in the series),[13] for the shift in vampiric diets that this book has been tracing, blood bags are a key addition that not only expands the range of food behaviours available to vampires, but diversifies what can be considered ethical consumption practices.

Consumption of human blood drawn from blood bags can be considered ethical because no human has been harmed or killed. As Damon remarks, 'there's nothing wrong with partaking in a healthy diet of human blood from a blood bank [because] you're not actually killing anyone' ('Under Control' 00:01:43–49).[14] This makes it a 'more socially responsible [dietary] model' of human-blood consumption (McMahon-Coleman and Weaver 156), one that removes the need for vampires to exploit and 'use [humans like] livestock' (*Dark Reunion* 423). This adds to the sense that a diet of donated human blood establishes a more ethical and less hierarchical feeding arrangement between species, and so updates the novels' depiction of blood-sharing for the Anthropocene.

The moral standpoint of vampires like Louis, Edward and Stefan (whose choice to subsist on a diet of animal blood stems from a moral consideration for human life) is also shared by those vampires who choose to subsist on donated blood. For instance, a deep respect for human life and desire to spare human suffering leads Lexi to move to a diet of donated blood. Importantly, she has tried to live on animal blood. As she tells Stefan, 'I tried the animal diet. Lasted three weeks' ('162 Candles' 00:14:10–13), before settling on donated human blood. For Lexi (as for those other vampires led by morality who make the same choice) a diet of donated blood provides a convenient middle ground: she is able to maintain her ethical stance while slaking her natural thirst. In this regard, a

[12] In actions such as this, the use of vampires in the television series and contemporary vampire fiction as a 'metaphor for a persecuted racial minority' (Houston 271) is clearly discernible and demands further analysis from critics.

[13] When Stefan struggles with his urge for human blood in later seasons, Caroline becomes his self-appointed 'sober sponsor' ('The Cell' 00:04:18). She also helps Elena learn to control her bloodlust ('The Memorial' 00:29:41–31:38).

[14] This view is in line with the stance of ethical vegetarianism, which rejects the slaughter of animals.

choice to consume human blood drawn from blood bags is at the same time a choice to not feed directly on or kill humans. So, while feeding on donated blood is not strictly 'vegetarian' in Meyer's understanding of the term as these vampires are still consuming human blood, vampires like Lexi are nevertheless motivated by the same ethical principles that drive Stefan, the Cullens and even Louis.

A diet of donated human blood also makes possible the same types of inter-species relations as a diet of animal blood. Damon is a good example of this. In early episodes, his diet of stolen human blood underwrites his depiction as the 'bad' brother. In the teasers, he is often shown preying on (and tormenting) couples in romantic situations, further proof that in the television series love and the drinking of human blood are incompatible.[15] Over time, however, he adopts a diet of donated blood. He chooses this owing to his growing love for Elena, as well as his desire to stay in Mystic Falls. Importantly, choosing this diet allows Damon to do all that: become settled, befriend Elena and other humans like Alaric and Caroline's mother, Sheriff Liz Forbes (who is also a member of the Founder's Council), and in later seasons, even gain Elena's love. These developments suggest that a diet of donated blood is a close equivalent to a diet of animal blood, if not by means then in ends: both provide alternate sources of blood for the vampire to subsist on, and both enable species (vampires and humans) to evolve new ways of engaging with each other. This makes still more prominent the link, established in previous vampire texts, between diet and the kinds of human-vampire relations that can be developed.

A diet of donated blood can support these developments because vampires who subsist on donated blood, just like vampires who consume animal blood, are 'no longer on the prowl for human prey' and, therefore, 'no longer pose a fatal threat to [the] human population' (Gerhards 246–47). Its power to foster inter-species relations can also be related in part to the long and remarkably patriotic history of blood donation in the United States. In her history of the American Red Cross, Marina Levina writes that since World War 2, 'narratives of patriotism, nationalism, and unity [have been used] to solicit donations' (16) from the American public. During the war, blood donation was pitched as a home front activity that civilians could engage in, with 'blood donation [the] moral equivalent to spilling [one's own] blood on the battlefield' (19). This created a 'narrative of community participation and sacrifice' around blood

---

[15] See, for example, 'Pilot' and 'The Night of the Comet'.

donation, which enabled it to transcend its material function as a medical aid and become a symbolic process capable of creating 'a unified social body' (19). After the war had ended, blood donation was thought to achieve the same end through exclusion: certain groups of people (for example, African Americans and homosexual men) were not allowed to donate blood, owing to the risk it was thought their blood posed to the American social body. To a certain extent, the television series draws upon these longstanding links between blood donation and community building. In the television series, donated blood enables certain kinds of outsiders (vampires) to be included. Although vampires like Damon and Lexi are stealing (and drinking), thus not donating blood, the process ends with the same result: they can become a part of Mystic Falls' society.[16]

Importantly, blood bags allow for the incorporation of a vampire's difference *as a* difference. Unlike in *Twilight*, in which the Cullens' vampire nature is all but erased (Scott 126), vampires in the television series who consume donated human blood are accepted for what they are: creatures who survive by drinking human blood. As Damon tells Elena, 'we're vampires Elena. We need human blood to survive. We're predators, not puppies' ('Break on Through' 00:3:55–59). The series 'never shies away from' this position (Brennan 8). However, acceptance of vampires is not universal. Amongst humans who are aware of the existence of vampires, some, like members of the Founder's Council, reject all vampires, regardless of their diet. But those who recognize the difference between diets and notions of morality and ethics flagged by that difference can and often do accept vampires who have made the choice to consume human blood drawn from blood bags. Thus, in the television series, at least to a certain extent, the vampire's biological impulse is not demonized as it is in *Twilight*, nor blocked with microchips and magic, as it is on occasion in *Buffy*. Instead, a different pathway is opened up in which the vampire's thirst can be sated as it was intended to, but in a way that, for the most part, supports coexistence between vampires and humans. The television series maintains the possibility that some humans can accept vampires (and vice versa) and choose to live together peacefully, if vampires make the

[16] As Megan Connor observes in her MA thesis '"Anne Rice for Kids" and Twilight for TV: Young Adult Media Franchising and the Vampire Diaries' (University of Wisconsin-Milwaukee, 2015) 'the series even partnered with the American Red Cross in the weeks prior to the show's premiere for a *Vampire Diaries* blood drive, which targeted young adults on high school and college campuses around the country' (60).

right dietary choices. This anticipates the broader acceptance of vampires as seen in *Mysteries*, but not in *True Blood*, as I will discuss.

Finally, with the addition of blood bags to the foods available to its vampires, the television series strengthens the link, established in *Twilight*, between the contemporary vampire's diet and sustainable eating practices. As the previous chapter showed, the Cullens' hunting practices are explicitly linked to an awareness of the ecological devastation that is caused by the use of animals as a source of food for humans and vampires. That same awareness is evident in Damon's albeit flippant observation that his diet of donated blood 'might actually be more ethical and sustainable than Stefan's rampant depletion of the forest ecosystem' (McFarland-Taylor 152). His observation carries weight. Insofar as no animal is killed to provide this dietary alternative, the ecosystem *is* left untouched. One imagines that critics who took aim at the Cullens' hunting practices as 'anything but green-friendly' (Myers-Smith qtd. in Mc Elroy and Mc Elroy 85) would agree with Damon. In Myers-Smith's view, 'if Meyer really wanted to have her … vampires live out their interminable lives in harmony with bona fide vegetarian principles, all she had to do … was to have them … head down to the local blood bank for a quick, intravenous fix' (qtd. in Mc Elroy and Mc Elroy 86). Myers-Smith has a point. A diet of donated blood both minimises the harm done to humans via the vampire's traditional feeding method (McMahon-Coleman and Weaver 156) and any environmental harm brought on by vampiric vegetarianism. (This is true of some vampires like Stefan, whose diet and feeding habits are guided only by a desire to protect human life. The same cannot be said for the Cullens.) Whether or not this is a *more* sustainable dietary model, in closer alignment with 'bona fide vegetarian principles' as Myers-Smith suggests, is open for debate (qtd. in Mc Elroy and Mc Elroy 86). It is plausible to argue that a diet of donated human blood is a step on from a diet of animal blood, offering a more sustainable, less destructive way of supporting (vampiric) life. It might also be possible to argue that a diet of donated human blood is neither better nor worse than a diet of animal blood; but rather the value of donated human blood lies simply in its introduction of another sustainable, as well as ethical, dietary alternative to traditional vampiric feeding behaviours. Either way, the addition of donated human blood to the television series' vampires' menu both registers, and responds to, the call for more conscious consumer practices that are increasingly necessary in the

Anthropocene.[17] At the very least, it fuels the series' 'ongoing' 'debates about consumption ethics' on-screen and in fan forums (McFarland-Taylor 152–53).

In sum, the television series offers a salient case study in two areas. One the one hand, in the changes that the television series makes to the story told in the novels, particularly regarding the vampire's animal-blood diet, one finds a timely update of the early 1990s novels that is attuned to our twenty-first century context and concerns. On the other, we get a good working example of the extent to which vampire fiction has changed over the last two decades, partly because of the influence exerted by *Twilight*, and partly, as I have been arguing, in response to the growing dangers to human life posed by the Anthropocene. Further, in the television series' diversification of the vampire's existing diet of human and/or animal blood through the introduction of donated human blood as another viable (and sustainable) source of nourishment that is accepted by some humans, we find a step towards *True Blood* and the invention of a synthetic blood drink for vampires. Made in Japanese labs, this vegan blood alternative is the next logical step in the genre's contemporary preoccupation with diet, one that offers the possibility of an even less binary relation between humans and vampires.

Works Cited

Alexander, Jenny. 'The Case of the Green Vampire: Eco-celebrity, Twitter and Youth Engagement.' *Celebrity Studies*, vol. 4, no 3, Nov. 2013, pp. 353–68.

Brennan, Sarah. 'Women Who Love Vampires Who Eat Women: Gender Dynamics and Interspecies Dating in Mystic Falls.' *A Visitor's Guide to Mystic Falls: Your Favourite Authors on The Vampire Diaries*, edited by Red and Vee, BenBella Books, 2010.

Bridgeman, Mary. 'Forged in Love and Death: Problematic Subjects in *The Vampire Diaries*.' *The Journal of Popular Culture*, vol. 46, no. 1, Feb. 2013, pp. 3–19.

Carter, Kristen. 'How *The Vampire Diaries* Wronged Bonnie Bennett.' *Black Girl Nerds*, blackgirlnerds.com/vampire-diaries-wronged-bonnie-bennett/. Accessed 19 Nov. 2019.

---

[17] The series' eco-friendly attitude is also evident in its eco-friendly set and cast. For more on this, see Alexander; McFarland-Taylor 153; and Malkin.

Crawford, Joseph. *The Twilight of the Gothic? Vampire Fiction and the Rise of the Paranormal Romance.* Wales UP, 2014. *JSTOR*, www.jstor.org/stable/j.ctt9qhjcp.

Day, William Patrick. *Vampire Legends in Contemporary American Culture: What Becomes a Legend Most.* Kentucky UP, 2015. *ProQuest Ebook Central*, ebook-central.proquest.com/lib/unimelb/detail.action?docID=1915342.

Dudek, Debra. *The Beloved Does Not Bite: Moral Vampires and the Humans Who Love Them.* Routledge, 2018. *Taylor and Francis Online*, https://doi.org/10.4324/9781315225425.

Frank, Alexandra C. 'All-Consuming Passions: Vampire Foodways in Contemporary Film and Television.' *What's Eating You? Food and Horror on Screen*, edited by Cynthia J. Miller et al., Bloomsbury Academic, 2017, pp. 339–52.

George, Sam, and Bill Hughes, editors. *Open Graves, Open Minds: Representations of the Vampire and the Undead from the Enlightenment to the Present Day*, Manchester UP, 2013. *JSTOR*, www.jstor.org/stable/j.ctt18mvm36.

Gerhards, Lea. 'Vampires "On a Special Diet": Identity and the Body in Contemporary Media Texts.' *Dracula and the Gothic in Literature, Pop Culture and the Arts*, edited by Isabel Ermida, BRILL, 2015, pp. 237–58. *ProQuest Ebook Central*, ebookcentral.proquest.com/lib/unimelb/detail.action?docID=4007474.

Houston, Lynn Marie. 'Biting Critiques: Paranormal Romance and Moral Judgement in *True Blood, Twilight* and *The Vampire Diaries*.' *A Critique of Judgment in Film and Television*, edited by Silke Panse and Dennis Rothermel, Palgrave Macmillan, 2014, pp. 269–88. *Springer Link*, https://doi.org/10.1057/9781137014184.

Jeanna, Shannon. 'The Problematic Treatment of People of Colour on *The Vampire Diaries*.' 17 Jul. 2015, shannonjeanna.wordpress.com/2015/07/17/the-problematic-treatment-of-people-of-color-on-the-vampire-diaries/. Accessed 19 Nov. 2019.

'Kevin Williamson Talks About the Future of "The Vampire Diaries."' *Los Angeles Times*, 29 Oct. 2009, latimesblogs.latimes.com/showtracker/2009/10/kevin-williamson-talks-about.html. Accessed 10 Feb. 2018.

Leavenworth, Maria Lindgren, and Malin Isaksson. *Fanged Fan Fiction: Variations on Twilight, True Blood and the Vampire Diaries.* McFarland, 2013. *ProQuest Ebook Central*, ebookcentral.proquest.com/lib/unimelb/detail.action?docID=1286896.

Levina, Marina. *Pandemics and the Media.* Peter Lang, 2015.

Lewis, Rachel Charlene. 'Julie Plec Continues "The Vampire Diaries" Tradition of Black Women Saving White Women.' *Bitch Media*, 22 July 20, www.bitchmedia.org/article/megan-thee-stallion-bonnie-bennett-the-vampire-diaries. Accessed 19 Nov. 2019.

'Love Hurts.' *Nylon Magazine*, Feb 2010, www.nylon.com/articles/vampire-diaries-nylon-interviews. Accessed 22 June 2022.

Malkin, Marc. 'Ian Somerhalder's Quest to Turn Vampires Green.' *E! News*, 17 Apr. 2012, www.eonline.com/uk/news/308494/ian-somerhalder-s-quest-to-turn-vampires-green. Accessed 26 Mar. 2019.

Mc Elroy, James, and Emma Catherine Mc Elroy. 'Eco-Gothics for the Twenty-First Century.' *The Twilight Mystique: Critical Essays on the Novels and Films*, edited by Amy M. Clarke and Marijane Osborn, McFarland, 2010, pp. 80–91.

McFarland-Taylor, Sarah. *Ecopiety: Green Media and the Dilemma of Environmental Virtue*. NYU Press, 2019.

McMahon-Coleman, Kimberly. 'Myriad Mirrors: Doppelgangers and Doubling in The Vampire Diaries.' George and Hughes, pp. 210–24.

McMahon-Coleman, Kimberly, and Roslyn Weaver. *Werewolves and Other Shapeshifters in Popular Culture: A Thematic Analysis of Recent Depictions*. McFarland, 2012. *ProQuest Ebook Central*, ebookcentral.proquest.com/lib/unimelb/detail.action?docID=928922.

Nicol, Rhonda. '"You Were Such a Good Girl When You Were Human": Gender and Subversion in *The Vampire Diaries*.' *Gender in the Vampire Narrative*, edited by Amanda Hobson and U. Melissa Anyiwo, BRILL, 2016, pp. 145–60. *ProQuest Ebook Central*, ebookcentral.proquest.com/lib/unimelb/detail.action?docID=4737016.

Nuñez, Kismet. 'Loving Vampire Diaries: Why History, Slavery and Race in Fandom Matters.' *WordPress*, 2 Dec. 2011, nunezdaughter.wordpress.com/2011/12/02/loving-vampire-diaries-why-history-slavery-and-race-in-fandom-matters/. Accessed 19 Nov. 2019.

Punter, David. *The Literature of Terror: A History of Gothic Fictions from 1975 to the Present Day*. Vol 2, Addison Wesley Longman Ltd, 1996.

Rodman, Sarah. 'Charmed by the Dark Side—With "Vampire Diaries," The CW Banks on Blood, Lust, and the Sexy Undead.' *Boston Globe*, 8 Sept. 2009. ProQuest, www.proquest.com/docview/405189648?accountid=12372.

Scott, Lindsey. 'Crossing Oceans of Time: Stoker, Coppola, and the "New Vampire" Film.' George and Hughes, pp. 113–30.

Smith, L. J. *The Vampire Diaries: The Awakening and The Struggle*, 1991. HarperTeen, 2007.

———. *The Vampire Diaries: The Fury and Dark Reunion*. 1991. HarperTeen, 2007.

———. *The Vampire Diaries: The Hunters: Phantom*. HarperTeen, 2011a.

———. *The Vampire Diaries: The Return: Midnight*. HarperTeen, 2011b.

———. *The Vampire Diaries: The Hunters: Destiny Rising*. HarperTeen, 2012a.

———. *The Vampire Diaries: The Hunters: Moonsong*. HarperTeen, 2012b.

———. *The Vampire Diaries: The Return: Nightfall*. HarperTeen, 2009.

———. *The Vampire Diaries: The Return: Shadow Souls*. HarperTeen, 2010.

——— *The Vampire Diaries: The Salvation: Unmasked*. HarperTeen, 2014.

———. *The Vampire Diaries: The Salvation: Unseen*. HarperTeen, 2013a.

———. *The Vampire Diaries: The Salvation: Unspoken*. HarperTeen, 2013b.

Sollosi, Mary. 'How *Twilight* Changed Pop Culture.' *Entertainment Weekly*, 21 Nov. 2018, ew.com/movies/2018/11/21/twilight-anniversary-impact/. Accessed 23 Mar. 2018.

Subramanian, Janani, and Jorie Lagerwey. 'Teen Terrors: Race, Gender, and Horrifying Girlhood in *The Vampire Diaries*.' *Reading in the Dark: Horror in Children's Literature and Culture*, edited by Jessica R. McCort, Mississippi UP, 2016, pp. 180–200.

Thomas, Ebony Elizabeth. *The Dark Fantastic: Race and the Imagination from Harry Potter to the Hunger Games*. New York UP, 2019.

Toff, Benjamin. '"Vampire Diaries" Makes its Mark.' *The New York Times*, 11 Sept. 2009, www.nytimes.com/2009/09/12/arts/television/12arts-VAMPIREDIARI_BRF.html?searchResultPosition=1. Accessed 26 Mar. 2018.

Williamson, Milly. *The Lure of the Vampire: Gender, Fiction and Fandom from Bram Stoker to Buffy*. Wallflower Press, 2005.

———. 'Television, Vampires and the Body: Somatic Pathos.' *Mysterious Bodies*, special issue of *Intensities: Journal of Cult Media*, edited by Rayna Denison and Mark Jancovich, vol. 4, autumn/winter, 2007, intensitiescultmedia.files.wordpress.com/2012/12/williamson-television-vampires-and-the-body.pdf.

Film and TV

'Bad Moon Rising.' Directed by Andrew Chambliss. *The Vampire Diaries*, season 2, episode 3, The CW, 23 Sept. 2010. *Stan*, https://www.stan.com.au/.

'The Birthday.' Directed by John Behring. *The Vampire Diaries*, season 3, episode 1, The CW, 15 Sept. 2011. *Stan*, https://www.stan.com.au/.

'Break on Through.' Directed by Lance Anderson. *The Vampire Diaries*, season 3, episode 17, The CW, 22 Mar. 2012. *Stan*, https://www.stan.com.au/.

'The Cell.' Directed by Chris Grismer. *The Vampire Diaries*, season 5, episode 9, The CW, 5 Dec. 2013. *Stan*, https://www.stan.com.au/.

'Friday Night Bites.' Directed by John Dahl. *The Vampire Diaries*, season 1, episode 3, The CW, 24 Sept. 2009. *Stan*, https://www.stan.com.au/.

'Haunted.' Directed by Earnest Dickenson. *The Vampire Diaries*, season 1, episode 7, The CW, 29 Oct. 2009. *Stan*, https://www.stan.com.au/.

'Klaus.' Directed by Joshua Butler. *The Vampire Diaries*, season 2, episode 19, The CW, 21 Apr. 2011. *Stan*, https://www.stan.com.au/.

'The Memorial.' Directed by Rob Hardy. *The Vampire Diaries*, season 4, episode 2, The CW, 18 Oct. 2012. *Stan*, https://www.stan.com.au/.

'Miss Mystic Falls.' Directed by Marcos Siega. *The Vampire Diaries*, season 1, episode 19, The CW, 22 Apr. 2010. *Stan*, https://www.stan.com.au/.

'The Night of the Comet.' Directed by Marcos Siega. *The Vampire Diaries*, season 1, episode 2, 17 Sept. 2009. *Stan*, https://www.stan.com.au/.

'162 Candles.' Directed by Rick Bota. *The Vampire Diaries*, season 1, episode 8, The CW, 5 Nov. 2009. *Stan*, https://www.stan.com.au/.

'Pilot.' Directed by Marcos Siega. *The Vampire Diaries*, season 1, episode 1, The CW, 10 Sept. 2009. *Stan*, https://www.stan.com.au/.

'The Reckoning.' Directed by John Behring. *The Vampire Diaries*, season 3, episode 5, The CW, 13 Oct. 2011. *Stan*, https://www.stan.com.au/.

'Rose.' Directed by Liz Friedlander. *The Vampire Diaries*, season 2, episode 8, The CW, 4 Nov. 2010. *Stan*, https://www.stan.com.au/.

Twilight. Directed by Catherine Hardwicke, Summit Entertainment, 2008.

'Under Control.' Directed by David Von Ancken. *The Vampire Diaries*, season 1, episode 18, The CW, 15 Apr. 2010. *Stan*, https://www.stan.com.au/.

CHAPTER 6

Vegan Vampires: *The Southern Vampire Mysteries* and *True Blood*

Abstract This chapter turns to texts in which vampires have available to them synthetic blood, namely, Charlaine Harris's *The Southern Vampire Mysteries* and its television adaptation *True Blood*. This commodity, manufactured in Japanese labs and marketed to vampires as True Blood, expands still further the possibilities for human-vampire relations while making it possible for the vegetarian vampire, discussed in earlier chapters, to become vegan. However, *Mysteries* and *True Blood* represent in very different ways the possibilities that these developments open for inter-species relations. The first half of this chapter focuses on the *Mysteries* novels, which are optimistic about the possibility of inter-species relations opened by synthetic blood. In contrast, *True Blood* brings to the fore the societal tensions inflamed by inter-species relations, caused by prejudice, racism, and speciesism, which in *Mysteries* are largely left in the background. The second half of the chapter discusses these tensions which stymie the novels' optimistic developments and suggests that there are issues that must be addressed before humanity will be capable of a 'greater moral-ethical response, and responsibility, to non-human [and inhuman] life forms' (Nayar 8).

Keywords *The Southern Vampire Mysteries* • *True Blood* • Synthetic blood • Veganism • Racism

As Chaps. 4 and 5 have argued, in twenty-first-century vampire texts we find stories that suggest what it might look like to live, act and eat with greater ethical responsibility and care for other (plant and animal) life forms. Charlaine Harris's *The Southern Vampire Mysteries* (2001–13) and Alan Ball's television adaptation *True Blood* (2008–14) continue this trend with a key difference. Rather than slaking their thirst on animal or donated human blood, Harris's vampires have a newly developed synthetic blood at their disposal. Made in Japanese laboratories and sold under a variety of hemoderivative names, such as Life Flow, Life Support, and True Blood (TruBlood in *True Blood*),[1] this synthetic product is marketed as a beverage able to meet all the nutritional needs of a vampire. As a result, vampires have 'come out of the coffin (as they laughingly put it)' (*Dead Until Dark* 1)—a phrase that has encouraged some critics to read the series as an allegory for gay rights (Brace and Arp; Elliot-Smith; Smith 203–06; Wright 57)[2]—and become part of human society. No longer merely vegetarians, the vampires who consume True Blood, rather than animal or donated human blood, are arguably vegan, as synthetic blood contains no human or animal biomaterial (Wright 58).

This chapter takes synthetic blood and its impact on human-vampire relations as its chief focus, as represented in *Mysteries* and *True Blood*. The former is optimistic about the possibility of inter-species relations opened by synthetic blood. In contrast, the latter brings to the fore the societal tensions inflamed by inter-species relations, caused by prejudice, racism and speciesism, which, although present in *Mysteries,* are largely left in the background. In *True Blood*, the prominence of these tensions makes it seem much less likely that synthetic blood will be able to reshape human-vampire relations for the better.

Although the reasons for this shift are complex, the changes that *True Blood* makes to *Mysteries'* narrative arguably owe something to its socio-political context. Two months after *True Blood* premiered in September 2008, Barack Obama became America's first black president. For many, Obama's ascension 'initially signalled a coming of age in American politics whereby African Americans could dare share in his "audacity of hope" in achieving visible and meaningful equality'. In reality, his election provoked a 'rhetoric [of] extreme patriotism and racism', revealing the many ways in

---

[1] For a discussion of the significance of this change, see Crawford 261 and Chaplin 49.

[2] Ball has dismissed such readings, stating that as a 'gay [man] myself, I'm not going to say gay people are blood-sucking monsters' (Harrington and Ball 108).

which (white) Americans were aggressively against his 'vision of a plural society' (Ní Fhlainn 215). Alan Ball's decision to bring to the fore the tensions of race and racism, and to centre its retelling of *Mysteries'* narrative around such issues, can be seen as reflecting those same tensions brought into prominence by Obama's two terms in office (Gelder 413; Marrati 981–82; Smith 200).

In the first *Mysteries* novels, optimism around synthetic blood's ability to reshape human-vampire relations for the better is arguably a response to the socio-political context in which these books were written. Five months after the first novel was published, George W. Bush became America's 43rd President. America's Religious Right, which experienced growth towards the end of the second term in office of his predecessor, Bill Clinton (the result of efforts to 'rehabilitate the persistent rumours about [Clinton's] ... moral slippages' [206]), 'gained a significant foothold' in Bush's America. The new President's 'administration ... promoted abstinence-only sex education' in schools 'with no permission to discuss contraception and safe sex practices' and 'severely compromised and/or actively defunded' 'many contraceptive initiatives' (206, 207). Harris's decision to centre her novels around the development of synthetic blood can be seen as 'a reflexive counter-narrative to George W. Bush's 'increasingly conservative [and I would add religious] America' in favour of 'liberal scientific discourse and technological progress' (Ní Fhlainn 12, 175).

The novels were also arguably influenced by advances in biotechnology in the late 1990s and early 2000s, such as America's genetically modified food crop boom (Ackerman) and preliminary work exploring the possibility of in vitro (lab-grown) meat. For the proponents of biotechnology, these developments were a solution to world hunger, sustainable farming practices, remaking human-animal relations (Dennis and Witchard; Hopkins and Dacey; Metcalf) and so on. But as the twenty-first century progressed, issues affecting genetically modified food came to light, such as cost and production difficulties (McGregor and Houston 12), adverse environmental flow-on effects (Lynch and Pierrehumbert) and the realisation that biotechnological advances, such as lab-grown meat, heighten rather than remove egregious animal abuses (Alvaro; Miller; Poirier and Russell). For these reasons, the early optimism around biotechnology's potential to remake the world's food systems waned. This, coupled with rising racial tensions, can be said to be a source of *True Blood*'s pessimism regarding diet's ability to reshape human-vampire relations.

The last volume of *Mysteries* was published in 2013, so this growing scepticism about the promises of biotechnology and rising racial tensions are also part of the context in which later volumes were written and the series as a whole was received. This can be discerned in the later volumes' depiction of America's anti-assimilationist response to werewolves and were-creatures (*Dead in the Family* 76–77, 233–34, 271)[3] and references to racial segregation within supernatural communities (*Deadlocked* 197).

These differences between the contexts in which *Mysteries* and *True Blood* were first conceived are significant for the trajectories of both series. In the following sections, I will argue that, as they unfold (insofar as they are concerned with human-vampire relations that are opened by synthetic blood), the novels and TV series both respond to and therefore reflect the changing socio-cultural and political conditions of their time. The first half of this chapter explores the *Mysteries* novels, their depiction of synthetic blood and the types of relationships between humans and vampires that it opens up or at least makes possible. It argues that these novels refract the optimism of the late twentieth and early twenty-first century regarding humanity's ability to change for the better our relations with other species and to live more sustainably with the environment.[4] It then turns to consider how these aspects are taken up, revised or rejected in *True Blood*.

Charlaine Harris's *The Southern Vampire Mysteries*

Dead Until Dark begins with vampire Bill walking into Merlotte's Bar and Grill, a non-descript family bar in the rural, northern Louisiana town of Bon Temps, where the novels (and TV series) are set. He sits down at a table and orders 'the bottled synthetic blood'. Unfortunately for Bill, Merlotte's does not have any. Sam, the owner of the bar, and a shifter (he can turn into any animal, though he favours dogs), has 'some on order', but it will not arrive until 'next week' (3). So Bill orders a glass of wine, which he does not drink. This leads Sookie Stackhouse, a telepathic

[3] On this point Kevin J. Wetmore Jr. disagrees, instead arguing America's anti-assimilationist response to werewolves and were-creatures owes to post-9/11 representations of werewolves as terrorists. He remarks 'because [werewolves] can pass as human but are capable of transformation into violent being[s]', they are 'the violent other already hiding within society' (60).

[4] Here my argument differs from Dale Hudson's, who claims supernaturalism, and not diet, in *True Blood* offers a model for imagining better relations with 'species other than humans' (663).

half-human, a half-fae waitress at Merlotte's and the narrator of the story, to assume that he is looking for 'some company' (17). But as Jennifer Carter suggests, Bill does so because his 'goal is to mainstream'. He 'understands' that ordering an alcoholic drink is standard behaviour in a bar and 'so when he orders wine … it's in an attempt to fit in' (28).

This opening scene establishes, as one critic has described it, the 'cosy' premise of *Mysteries'* world (Crawford 250), namely that, thanks to the invention of synthetic blood, vampires have been able to become part of human society. Now 'everyday tasks, such as shopping for food in grocery stores and socializing in bars, [can be and] are performed by vampires … too' (Gerhards 249). This marks a significant departure from previous representations of the vampire. In *Mysteries'* fictional world, vampires are not McGuffins nor do they 'work hard to integrate with the human world unrecognised as vampires' (Mutch 85), as the Cullens in *Twilight* and some vampires in *The Vampire Diaries* strive to do. Instead, *Mysteries'* vampires are trying to fit in with human society while asserting their difference. This makes still more prominent the link, established in previous vampire texts, between diet and the kinds of human-vampire relations that can be developed.

The availability of synthetic blood also enables the enfranchisement of vampires. This development is not universal: America, England, Canada, Japan and Switzerland accept vampires as 'equal citizens' (*Club Dead* 5); but others have 'pronounced vampires nonhuman and urged their citizens to kill vampires on sight' (*Definitely Dead* 77). Nevertheless, the extension of a vampire's legal rights is an important and arguably logical next step from the social exchanges between species made possible when vampires adopt a diet of animal or donated blood.

Over *Mysteries'* 13 novels the extent of these rights is gradually revealed: vampires own homes, run lucrative businesses (predominately bars and nightclubs, owing to their nocturnal lifestyle), have homeowners and group insurance, and can legally marry humans. Bella and Edward also marry, but this is done without society's knowledge of Edward's condition. They also pay taxes. In *Living Dead in Dallas*, Sookie speculates that Congress only granted vampires 'the legal right to exist' to 'obligate them into paying taxes' (24). For Susan Chaplin, this suggests that legal rights are extended to vampires because money can be made out of them:

> at the point at which [vampires] come to make their demand for tolerance and civil rights, [they] already possess the type of subjectivity—premised

upon the capacity for legitimate economic production and consumption—
that a capitalist society recognizes as at least notionally valid. (80)

Congress appears to understand, as Sookie does, that 'any vampire worth
his salt could become wealthy', armed as they are with powers to control
human minds and therefore persuade humans to 'part with money, stock
tips or investment opportunities' (24). However, vampires can become
'good, productive economic subjects' that are taxable and thus tolerable
citizens, who 'work … earn … [and] consume' (Chaplin 80) like any other
American citizen, but *only* because of the availability of synthetic blood. As
Sookie observes in *Club Dead*, when vampires around the world announced
their existence 'the burden of this' fell on the development of synthetic
blood. This enabled vampires to claim that 'now we can come forward and
join with you in harmony. You are in no danger from us anymore. We
don't need to drink from you to live' (5). It is society's acceptance of this
claim that informs the decision to extend legal rights to vampires, which
in turn enables them to be taxed. Indeed, many of the successful vampire
businesses described in *Mysteries* revolve around vampire tourism of
sorts—vampire bars, nightclubs and, particularly in New Orleans, vampire-
related attractions—that draw in human business and, therefore, produce
taxable income. Diet, not money, underwrites *Mysteries*' assimilationist
narrative.

The success of vampire business ventures, linked as they are to a vampire's ability to become part of human society, owes something to the fact
that the blood they are now able to consume is not connected to notions
of race or species. Throughout history, humanity has made blood 'a cru-
cial metaphor for what it thinks of as racial identity' (Stevenson 144). As
John Allen Stevenson writes, 'blood is the essence that somehow deter-
mines all those other features—physical and cultural—that distinguish one
race from another' (144). In earlier texts, the vampire's diet of human
blood threatened what was thought to be the very basis of individual and
cultural identity.[5] In contrast, synthetic blood lacks 'all [the] symbolic
qualities and life-sustaining connotations' (Aldana Reyes 60) of true (i.e.
human) blood. Made in Japanese labs and containing no human or animal
genetic material, synthetic blood makes no assertion about race, class,

[5] Several critics have written at length on the anxieties aroused by blood in vampire fiction.
In addition to Stevenson, see, for example Aldana Reyes; Arata 630–33; Levina 61–77;
Stephanou, '"Ghastly Operation"' and *Reading*.

identity or species. Like so many other consumer products, True Blood is 'made in Japan' and the types of blood available are merely flavours (Bill's favourite is O positive). As a result, the usual fears that come with the vampire's human-blood diet (deracination, loss of identity and so on) can and for the most part are ignored in *Mysteries*, which makes the vampire's integration possible.

It is interesting to note that synthetic blood is also vegan, which is often described as the 'next step forward' from vegetarianism (Spencer 317).[6] Where the latter is 'by definition' limited to 'abstinence from meat-eating' (Quinn and Westwood 5), veganism is

> a philosophy and way of living which seeks to exclude—as far as is possible and practicable—all forms of exploitation of, and cruelty to, animals for food, clothing or any other purpose [such as entertainment or medical testing]; and by extension, promotes the development and use of animal-free alternatives for the benefits of animals, humans and the environment. In dietary terms it denotes the practice of dispensing with all products derived wholly or partly from animals. ('Definition of Veganism')

A vegan diet and lifestyle is the most thorough and all-encompassing rejection of the place conventionally assigned in human culture to the animal, as useable, exploitable and consumable 'in the service of ... the putative human well-being of a man' (Mallet 25). In the place of traditional human-animal interactions, a vegan diet and lifestyle holds 'animal and human rights [as] equally valuable' (Wright 9) and, in so doing, introduces a radically relational model with 'the unique, dissimilar, noninterchangeable [animal] other' (Rowley 80).

We can see these developments at work in *Mysteries'* construction of human-vampire relations. Although the dynamic is different—it is the prey (humans) extending legal rights to the predator (vampires) as opposed to the predator (humans) extending moral and ethical rights to the prey (animals)—synthetic blood nevertheless makes possible a relation between species based on equality and trust. This 'disrupts the heretofore oppositional either/or of the human/vampire species binary ... a relationship dependent upon the destruction of one species for the preservation of the other' (Wright 60). In *Mysteries*, this opens a world which is much larger

---

[6] The Vegan Society was formed at Leicester in 1944, owing to the disenfranchisement of vegan members of the Vegetarian Society, which 'refused to publicise the vegan view' because it was considered 'very extreme ... and anti-social' (Spencer 317).

than vampires and humans, in which there is a baroque medley of species and, therefore, also of inter-species relations.

To return to the rights extended to vampires by humans: vampires take communion in the Episcopal church (but they cannot be priests) (*Definitely Dead* 12); become police officers (*Definitely Dead* 177–78);[7] they even cross over into the worlds of fashion (*Dead as a Doornail* 130) and reality television (*Dead and Gone* 1–3). One even appears on *The Oprah Winfrey Show* (*Dead Until Dark* 21). There are airlines and boutique hotels designed to cater specifically to vampires (with blacked-out windows and holding areas for coffins), and Motel 6, a well-known real-life motel chain in America, has 'one vampire room at almost every location' (*All Together Dead* 117–18). Vampire law also becomes a burgeoning speciality area taught at universities (*Definitely Dead* 251); and there are even vampire newspapers, such as '*American Vampire*' and '*Fang* (the vamp version of *People*)' (*All Together Dead* 116, 139), which publish vampire-interest reports. What this list suggests, and the variety of species that appear in *Mysteries* confirms, is the incredible sense of multiculturalism or multispecies cosmopolitanism evoked by these novels, which is entirely absent in *Buffy*, *Twilight* and *The Vampire Diaries*—owing to the vampire's synthetic blood diet.

However, where vampires in these earlier texts drink animal blood out of a desire to 'do the right thing' (Wright 62), the same cannot be said of vampires in *Mysteries* (or *True Blood*). Moral or ethical consideration for humans does not play into the decision of vampires to adopt or adapt to a vegan diet. On the contrary, their vegan diets are the result of chance and political aspirations. Sookie says as much in *Dead as a Doornail*, when she notes that the synthetic blood drink consumed by vampires was originally created for 'ambulance companies and hospital emergency rooms' rather than vampires. She goes on to claim that 'the last thing the Japanese had expected when they'd developed synthetic blood was that its availability would bring vampires out of the realm of legend and into the light of fact' (6). This is not to say that the vampires in *Mysteries* do not care for humans; vampires are shown to be able to love humans (some even marry). Even

[7] That inclusion of vampires in the police force is particularly notable given that in *Buffy* the slayer effectively takes the law into her own hands in order to keep vampires from harming humans.

so, their love or care for humans is not universal,[8] and it is not love or care for humans or moral consideration of humans' right to not be fed that guides vampires to a vegan diet. Unlike Louis, Edward or Stefan, these vampires do not view feeding on humans as wrong (Wright 62); indeed, many still feed on willing human partners. As 'Bill reports ... the longer he remains a vampire, the harder it is for him to remember what it was like to be [and care for] a human' (Carter 25; *Living Dead in Dallas* 219–20). They are driven instead by a desire to become a part of human society and enjoy the same sorts of civil and legal rights as humans. As a consequence, the extent to which synthetic blood can remake species relations is limited. It opens the possibility, but not necessarily the reality, of a new world. The latter might be seen in Bon Temps, but it is less apparent in the larger world, as *True Blood* will make still more evident.

Nevertheless, in *Mysteries,* the vampire's synthetic diet is able to draw the contours of a new world because the majority of its vampires choose it. Although the turn to synthetic blood is not primarily driven by ethical considerations, vampires understand that in order to become a part of human society, they must forgo their preference for human blood. Tellingly, in *Dead as a Doornail,* Eric refers to the time when vampires 'considered ourselves [to be] better than humans, separate from humans' and had 'very much the same relationship to humans as humans have to say, cows' (214). He describes these views as 'the old ways' (217) and, in the present of *Mysteries,* only a handful of vampires, such as Franklin Mott, Mickey and Alexei, try to stick to them, something they are punished for (*All Together Dead* 268–70). The rest choose to adhere to 'the new vampire policy of only feeding from willing humans or synthetic blood' (*Definitely Dead* 202). This decision applies to public *and* private domains and is true of regular vampires such as Bill, Pam and Eric, all of whom are repeatedly shown to drink synthetic blood and stock a supply of this beverage in their fridges (*Club Dead* 1, 267; *Dead to the World* 55; *Dead Until Dark* 172). Vampire Kings and Queens also subsist on synthetic blood, as is revealed when Sookie enters Sophie Anne Leclerq's (the Queen of Louisiana) hotel suite and finds an empty bottle of synthetic blood lying beside her (*All Together Dead* 119). Even older, less mainstreamed

---

[8] In *Dead in the Family,* for example, when Alexei kills two black American men, Eric is more concerned by the potential political backlash caused by Alexei's actions, and the impact this might have on the vampire assimilation movement, than with the deaths of two humans (243).

vampires, such as Eric's maker, Appius Livius Ocella (an ancient Roman vampire), are clued into the political, social and cultural times and use blood drawn from willing humans to supplement their diet of synthetic blood.[9] This last point is all the more astounding given that Ocella ignores other changes, such as the criminalisation of pederasty. Unlike vegetarian vampires, *Mysteries'* vampires do not change their diets for ethical reasons, but they nevertheless respect and abide by human laws, and by choosing to slake their thirst on synthetic blood (or blood drawn from willing humans), they are able, like vegetarian vampires before them, to become a part of human society.[10]

Putting synthetic blood to one side for a moment, I want now to consider how the geographical setting of the *Mysteries* novels can be said to frame or at the very least foreground its optimism. As critics have argued, it is 'no coincidence that the [novels are] set in the Deep South' (Blayde and Dunn 33), in a state that has 'often been one of the most vociferous against extending rights to non-white ... humans' (Hudson 663).[11] But the South's racial history is not foregrounded in *Mysteries* (as it is in *True Blood*). On the contrary, the comparison between the South's racial past and *Mysteries'* multispecies present is 'made— and rejected—in the novels themselves' (Crawford 37n309). Joseph Crawford takes as an example the scene, in *Dead as a Doornail*, when Charles Twining (a black British vampire) attempts to kill Sookie, only to be detained and killed by the mostly white male crowd at Merlotte's (37n309). This may evoke, for some readers, the mob violence and prejudice of the South's racist past (and arguably still racist present); but before staking Charles, the crowd defers first to Sookie's judgement, who advises that they should 'call the police'

---

[9] In *Mysteries*, the category of 'willing humans' extends from prostitutes who 'specialize in vampires' ('who drink synthetic blood to keep [their] blood supply up' [*Dead Until Dark* 25]), to human partners (blood and sex is conflated in *Mysteries* as acceptable), and then to state-sanctioned (*Dead Ever After* 49) and privatised registries where willing human donors can sign up to be fed on by a vampire (*Definitely Dead* 202).

[10] Critics like Bruce McClelland and Aspasia Stephanou read the vampire's consumption of synthetic blood in less positive terms and argue that synthetic blood is nothing more than a capitalist trap presented by mankind to vampires with a view to eliminating them. See Aldana Reyes 60–61; McClelland 83, 87; Stephanou, *Reading* 126–27. For a counterpoint, see Wright 60–62.

[11] Many critics have written at length on the socio-political importance of the series' Louisianan setting. See, for example, Woolfork, and for a particularly insightful analysis of the setting, see Hudson.

(289), and then to Charles's plea to 'end it' as he 'can't abide jails' (290). When Charles's wish is granted, Sookie remarks that,

> of course, it was tempting to think this was an echo of the terrible old days, when black men had been lynched if there was even a rumour they'd winked at a white woman. But you know, the simile just didn't hold. Charles was a different spade, true. But he'd been guilty as hell of trying to kill me. I would have been a dead woman ... if the men of Bon Temps hadn't intervened. (290)

This is not to say that *Mysteries* evokes a world without racism. Although Sookie may dismiss the simile, she nonetheless acknowledges that she is tempted to apply it to the scene; and parts of the narrative do deal with race and racism. The romantic relationship between Kevin (a white American male) and Kenya (a black American female), who are both officers in Bon Temps's police force, offers a clear example, as their families repeatedly refuse to accept their relationship (*Dead to the World* 295; *Dead Ever After* 142). The novels also make reference to segregation ('only white people seemed to want to' be buried by Mike Spencer, the town's white funeral director; 'people of colour chose to be buried at Sweet Rest' [*Dead Until Dark* 44]), red-lining, and racist policing (*Dead to the World* 197, 68). Sookie too only romances white supernatural creatures who identify as male (Hudson 664). Other aspects of the novel, as Ken Gelder has shown, engage the South's racial past, such as the antebellum homes either owned or inherited by the novels' predominantly white cast (Sookie, Bill and the Bellefleurs); their histories of slave-owing (Sookie's 'great-great-great-great grandfather' Jonas, 'had a house slave and a yard slave' [*Dead Until Dark* 53]); and links to the Confederacy (Bill was a Confederate soldier and Sookie's grandmother is a 'charter member of The Descendants of the Glorious Dead' [*Dead Until Dark* 26]) (412). Although Bill distances himself from his Confederate past, the presence of the latter, as Chaplin argues, 'hints at ... the community's celebration of and nostalgia for their pre-civil war [slave-owning] past' (78).[12]

---

[12] Parts of the novel also deal explicitly with homophobia. This comes to prominence through the character of Lafayette, the openly gay, black short-order cook at Merlotte's (*Dead Until Dark* 236; *Living Dead in Dallas* 8, 12–13, 16, 211) and minor characters such as the werewolf Adabelle (*Dead to the World* 119–20) and Sookie's fae cousin, Claude (*Dead Ever After* 324).

While present, these tensions and histories are not central to the narrative, which is, as Gelder suggests, more 'directly interested' in the 'dizzying array of supernatural species' that fills its pages and 'question[s] of [multispecies] assimilation' (411). His conclusion that this focus might be at least partially responsible for 'the downplaying of the significance of race, racial difference and racial discrimination' (413), with these things present but largely side-lined in the novels, is probably correct. By creating instead 'a "post-racial" vision of the South that is no longer especially interested in the realities of racial difference' (411), the novels are able to foreground the human-vampire relations made possible by vampires' adoption of a synthetic blood diet.

The same can be said for the representation, in *Mysteries*, of speciesism. Sookie makes several references to the discrimination that vampires face. In *Dead Ever After*, for example, when Sookie is suspected of murdering Arlene (a fellow waitress at Merlotte's), she notes that 'having a vampire as a witness to your whereabouts was not a glowing testimonial. Though they were now citizens of the United States, they were not treated or regarded like humans, not by a long shot' (142). As Sookie states elsewhere, Americans 'might have accepted the reality of vampires, but that didn't mean they liked undead Americans' (*Dead as a Doornail* 191). Even Sookie herself, as Dale Hudson observes, 'seems entangled' in speciesist behaviour when 'she refers to Bill as "vampire bill" a species-inflected moniker that troubles no one, as might racially inflected ones like "White Jason" and "Black Tara"' (666). The novels also track the emergence and radicalisation of the Fellowship of the Sun, 'an anti-vampire, anti-tolerance organization' that 'preached hatred and fear [of vampires] in its most extreme form' (*Definitely Dead* 125). However, in *Mysteries*, the Fellowship's actions are few and far between, occurring only a handful of times over the course of the 13 novels, always in other states and other cities (something that *True Blood* changes).[13]

To return to Bon Temps: discriminatory and violent speciesist practices, towards vampires, are not overtly present. Although some residents question Sookie's mixing with Bill, the majority accept their relationship and the wider undead community, who succeed in becoming a part of the 'economic and social flow of [Bon Temps'] society' (*All Together Dead* 17). The novels offer proof of the latter in the treatment that vampires

---

[13] In Dallas (*Living Dead in Dallas* 200–08) and Rhodes (*All Together Dead* 235, 284–91) for example.

receive at Merlotte's. The appearance of out-of-town vampires goes unremarked, save for 'a sideways glance by a few' (*Dead to the World* 12); two (Anthony Bolivar and Charles Twinning) even work there, as a short-order cook and a bartender respectively, with the latter proving popular among the regulars who tip him handsomely (*Living Dead in Dallas* 11; *Dead as a Doornail* 238). Some of these same customers *do* kill Charles in order to save Sookie, which suggests that species lines are ultimately maintained or, at the very least, defended if vampires break with the agreed-upon social contract (subsisting on synthetic blood and not killing humans). However, Charles's demise cannot be used to simply dismiss the broader significance of his employment, which otherwise draws attention to the possibility, if not actuality, of peaceful human-vampire relations present in Bon Temps (as long as vampires abide by the rules). No customers oppose his appointment, and the bar's revenue does not drop; on the contrary, 'the attraction of [the] new bartender' proves to be a lucrative draw that 'fill[s] Merlotte's with the optimistic and the curious' (*Dead as a Doornail* 168). 'We all get along here in Bon Temps', Sookie declares in *Dead and Gone* (13). This is a point made still more prominent by the town's acceptance of werewolves and other were-creatures when they make their existence known (9–12). Only Arlene, having been recently 'politically sensitized' by the Shreveport arm of Fellowship of the Sun, is upset (6, 13).

The lack of discriminatory or speciesist behaviour in Bon Temps could be read as suggesting that the town is beleaguered, surrounded by a larger world in which the divide between humans and vampires is hotly defended. Indeed, the handful of times where Sookie refers to the treatment of vampires in other parts of America and the globe draws attention to the fact that Bon Temps's largely tolerant attitude towards other species is anomalous.[14] In that regard, Bon Temps, situated as it is in the South, is arguably presented as 'forward thinking in [its] attitude toward multiculturalism and integration' (Mutch 85). By focusing on Bon Temps and its characters, even when seen against this more negative backdrop, *Mysteries* brings the inter-species possibilities opened by synthetic blood into the foreground. Here, at least, humans and vampires can co-exist, and are able to do so in relative peace and harmony thanks to synthetic blood.

---

[14] See *Club Dead* 5 and *Dead in the Family* 76–77, 105, 233–34, 266–71.

ALAN BALL'S *TRUE BLOOD*

True Blood brings the tensions left in the background of *Mysteries* (specie-sism, racism) into the foreground, which brings with them forces that stymie the possibilities for inter-species relations opened by synthetic blood. This is not to say that the possibility of human-vampire intimacy and integration is absent from *True Blood*. Its vampires' campaign for the Vampire Rights Amendment (VRA) to the American constitution, which would introduce the civil rights already extended to vampires in *Mysteries*; and at one stage in season three, the VRA is only two states away from rati-fication ('Everything is Broken'). Further, in the first season, Vermont legalises human-vampire marriage, the only state to do so ('You'll Be the Death of Me'). Nevertheless, at every turn, optimistic developments such as these appear to be brought to a halt by ingrained prejudice and, even more problematically, by what seems to be inscribed in the nature of vam-pires and humans.

The primal nature of vampires is revealed when they revert to tradi-tional diets, as seen in the third season when Russell Edgington, the vam-pire King of Mississippi, murders a news reporter on live television ('Everything is Broken'). His actions expose, as he proclaims, 'the true face of vampires' (00:55:08–12) as creatures who have no regard for human life and who, more importantly, 'drink the true blood. Blood that is', Russell explains, 'living, organic, and human', not synthetic (00:54:47–49). Whereas in *Mysteries* vampires who choose to feed on human blood (drawn from unwilling humans) are anomalous, in *True Blood* it is the vampires who choose to subsist on synthetic blood that are anomalous. Despite the frequent assurances given by Nan Flanagan (the spokesvampire and public face for the vampires' mainstreaming move-ment) that 'every member of our community is drinking synthetic blood' ('Strange Love' 00:01:33–36), only one vampire other than vampire Bill (Eddie Gauthier) is shown to subsist on synthetic blood.[15] Eric and Pam are unwilling to adopt a diet of synthetic blood. As Eric quips in one epi-sode, 'TruBlood … will keep you alive, but it will bore you to death'

---

[15] Even then, Bill is swayed by the teachings of the Sanguinista, the radical anti-mainstreaming vampire party. In the fifth season, he adopts a diet of only human blood, providing further proof of the show's haphazard stance on synthetic blood. Scenes depicting Bill's radicalisation can be found in the following episodes: 'In the Beginning', 'Gone, Gone, Gone' and 'Sunset'.

('Plais d'Amour' 00:03:37–41). Even Nan is eventually exposed as a vampire who consumes human blood ('Everything is Broken').

By showing vampires to be so widely and openly opposed to a diet of synthetic blood, *True Blood* illustrates the key issue raised by the unethical veganism adopted by vampires in *Mysteries*. Most of the vampires in *Mysteries* adopt a diet of synthetic blood because they want to enter mainstream human society. *True Blood*'s vampires, however, do not see this as advantageous. Malcolm, a member of Bill's former nest, neatly summarises the view held by most vampires, namely, that 'mainstreaming's for pussies' ('Burning House of Love' 00:30:54–56). Arguably this view derives from the fact that 'most vampires on *True Blood* are just as guilty of speciesism as human beings' (Blayde and Dunn 43). In the first season, for example, when vampire Bill stakes Longshadow (the show's sole Native American vampire and character) to save Sookie, he is punished severely by the Magister (the enforcer of vampire law in *True Blood*) for murdering 'a higher life form for the sake of your pet' ('I Don't Wanna Know' 00:29:55–59). As the Magister reminds Bill, 'humans exist to serve us, that is their only value' (00:31:04–06). Other vampires share the Magister's attitude. For example, Eric sees humans as 'pets' ('Scratches' 00:35:42) and Pam describes them as 'stupid cattle' ('To Love is to Bury' 00:00:16–8). These views are expressed still more forcefully when Russell asks his human audience 'why would we seek equal rights? You are not our equals. We will eat you after we eat your children' ('Everything is Broken' 00:55:18–37). These remarks suggest that veganism, along with the ethical relations between species that it embodies, will not be realised if ancient prejudices are carried into the present. At the very least, the link Russell draws between the consumption of human blood by vampires and their superiority over humans speaks eloquently to the need for an underlying ethical or moral imperative to guide relations between species. Synthetic blood might open the possibility of more harmonious relations between species, but it cannot by itself make these possibilities a reality.

In *True Blood*, vampires are not the only species who deem other species to be inferior. Humans are equally if not more intolerant of their others, even those who belong to the same species. This includes those who are not heterosexual (Amador 130), human (Blayde and Dunn) or white (Gelder 413–18; Hudson 663–76; Woolfork). The plight of the last category is most clearly conveyed through the character of Tara Thornton (Sookie's best friend) (Anyiwo; Hudson 674–76; Marrati 992;

Paquet-Deyris 193; Woolfork),[16] who plays the part of the 'volatile, disaffected black American' (Gelder 415)—in *Mysteries*, she is a successful white business owner, further proof of *True Blood*'s greater emphasis on race. Over the course of the series, she encounters police brutality; is magically enslaved by a wealthy, white woman in a plantation-style mansion (416); and in one episode, kidnapped, taken to Russell's 'antebellum mansion, tie[d] to a large bed and systematically rape[d]', whilst being told 'she smells "like spice"' (415). But even some of Tara's views recall racist anxieties, albeit now transposed to relations between species, such as her warning to Sookie that (human) women who have sex with vampires disappear ('Strange Love' 00:18:04–09). Tara is correct: some women who have sex with vampires do go missing. But the 'disappearance' that Tara speaks of 'is also metaphoric and racial' and recalls familiar fears of miscegenation: 'to have sex with the [racial] "other" is to risk the disappearance of racial purity' (Rabin, par. 9). Elsewhere, the series links racism and sexism, such as when Andy Bellefleur—a white male police officer who is, in the third season, acquitted for the shooting killing of an unarmed black male—is promoted to police chief over the more competent Kenya. Speaking about the injustice in Andy's appointment, Kenya quips that 'I guess the only way to get a promotion in this town is to drink like a fish, hallucinate farm animals, and kill a black man' ('9 Crimes' 00:19:40–47). These tensions are important, for if *Mysteries* can be said to reproduce a '"post-racial" vision of the South' (Gelder 414)—allowing the novels to foreground the possibility of a multicultural and multispecies world—*True Blood* shows that this is false or at the very least, still far out of reach.

While Sookie may claim in *Mysteries* that the parallel between race relations and species relations 'doesn't hold' (*Dead as a Doornail* 290), *True Blood* shows the analogy to be all too applicable as versions of the prejudices that divide races come to colour and therefore curb human-vampire relations. For instance, in season five, vampire lynch mobs, modelled after the Klu Klux Klan, operate in Bon Temps, replete with their own Dragon and masks ('Everybody Wants to Rule the World');[17] and in season six, in a scene that refracts the violence experienced by many black Americans, a news report shows a vampire being dragged to death behind a ute (pick-

---

[16] On this point Amador disagrees, instead arguing that Tara, through her friendly interactions with white characters such as Sookie, Adele, Jason and Sam, suggests the existence of a 'post-racial' South (125–29).

[17] See also 'Hopeless' and 'In the Beginning' for scenes depicting the lynch mob's actions.

up truck) ('The Sun'). The series also draws upon other notable examples of racial discrimination, most notably the Holocaust, when, in season six, vampires are rounded up by a state-run task force, interred in state-run prisons, starved and subjected to scientific studies and baiting ('Don't You Feel Me'). Louisiana's Governor even initiates the state's own version of a 'final solution' for vampires, with the creation and worldwide distribution of TruBlood contaminated with hepatitis V (a strain of the hepatitis virus that is lethal to vampires) and planned mass-killings of vampires through exposure to sunlight (Hughes 243). Unlike *Mysteries*, there is no side-lining these connections between race, racism and speciesism.

Pointing to the inclusion of Tyrese, an African American in Bon Temps's otherwise all-white vampire lynch mob, Dale Hudson sees evidence of speciesism 'diminish[ing]' (682) racism in *True Blood*. This is not the case. On the contrary, *True Blood* illustrates how Klan and Nazi-like racist actions, and the hatred and prejudices that inform them, can with little difficulty be repurposed to police the boundaries between species. Far from suggesting that one oppression diminishes or displaces another, *True Blood* suggests that 'all oppressions are linked and co-dependent, [and that] there can be no freedom from one form of oppression unless there is freedom from all of them' (Wright 17). This last point has significant implications for the Anthropocene. By showing racism and speciesism to be 'intersectional and codependently reinforcing' (Wright 15), *True Blood* arguably highlights the work towards broader inclusivity and equality that needs to be done before society can contemplate, let alone realise, truly equal relations with other species (vampires or nonhuman animals) and sustainable interactions with nature more broadly (Wright 8).

This final point comes to prominence through the character of Russell Edgington. Although Russell is one of *True Blood*'s 'most exaggeratedly Southern vampires', 'utterly secessionist [and] violently opposed to assimilation' (Gelder 413), he is also, with the exception of Bill, who recycles (McFarland-Taylor 156), the series' only environmentally conscious or 'green' vampire. His concern for the environment is conveyed through the many 'environmentally conscious monologues' (Atkinson 223) that he delivers in the third season. The most notable of these occurs during his appearance on live television, when he launches into a diatribe about mankind's consumer practices. Linking 'particular products to their material histories and to the destructive consequences of excessive consumption' (Atkinson 223), Russell berates his audience for 'global warming, perpetual war, toxic waste, child labor, torture [and] genocide', telling them 'that's a small price to pay for your SUVs and your flat screen TVs, your blood diamonds, your designer jeans, your absurd garish McMansions!' ('Everything Is Broken' 00:54:04–18).

However, his 'focused raging against the machine of human ecological destruction and excessive consumption' (Atkinson 227) is not motivated by an eco-friendly ethic, like the one adopted by the Cullens, which reflects a desire to live more sustainably with the planet and its multispecies inhabitants. Russell's motivations are self-serving: he only cares about the worsening state of the planet owing to its adverse effect on the smell and flavour of his human meals. As he reminisces to Eric, 'Do you remember how the air used to smell? How humans used to smell? How they used to taste?' ('I Gotta Right to Sing the Blues' 00:28:48–58). Again, where the Cullens' actions are peaceful, day-to-day acts of environmental practice, Russell's are violent, with genocidal tendencies. 'Throughout history', he tells Eric, 'I have aligned myself with or destroyed those humans in power, hoping to make a dent in mankind's race to oblivion' (00:28:34–42), citing Hitler and the Conquistadors as some of his allies. For Russell, such actions are justified in order to 'prevent humans from destroying the planet and themselves and thus our food source' ('Everything is Broken' 00:13:58–14:04).

It is not too far-fetched to suggest that Russell's environmentalism can be read as illustrating the ties between racism, speciesism and the climate crisis. Firstly, his acts of eco-piety are pointedly connected to the decimation and enslavement of peoples deemed to be other and inferior. His reference to the Conquistadors is especially telling in this regard, given their prominent role in the birth and growth of the African slave trade.[18] (The Portuguese were 'the first Europeans to sail along the Atlantic … in order to bring enslaved Africans back to Europe' and the 'first recorded slave ship to arrive in colonial America' was 'the Spanish ship *San Juan Bautista*' [Kendi 23, 38]). Secondly, Russell's actions are designed to ensure *vampires'* survival and quality of life; there is no cross-species care or responsibility towards humans guiding him in his self-appointed role as a manager of the planet.

---

[18] Although Hudson does not make this connection in his article, Russell's alliance with the Conquistadors is another example of how in *True Blood* the 'histories of enslavement from the Middle Passage through Jim Crow linger alongside histories of conquest/annexation from the Spanish Empire through the Republic of Texas' (670).

With regard to the latter point, one can discern in Russell's actions 'an uncomfortable truth of' human-earth and human-animal relations in 'the [A]nthropocene', 'especially for the brand of environmentalism that sees the earth as something to "save": any large-scale changes we make are designed mainly to ensure *humans'* survival, not the earth's or any of its billions of nonhuman inhabitants' (Mansbridge 217). We find in the exaggerated intersectionality of Russell's racism and environmentalism a truth regarding white/non-white relations in the Anthropocene, namely, that 'racial inequality ... is intertwined with our climate crisis' (Johnson). As Ayana Elizabeth Johnson has observed, '[p]eople of color disproportionately bear climate impacts, from storms to heat waves to pollution', the latter the result of 'fossil-fuelled power plants and refineries [being] disproportionately located in black neighbourhoods'. She adds the simple observation that if 'we don't work' at the same time on both racial injustice and climate change, 'we will succeed at neither'.

True Blood never 'goes as far as to advocate for [the environment or] environmental rights' (Hudson 677) and there is little evidence beyond Russell's comments that the television series is in any way interested in the climate crisis. However, one can nevertheless read his remarks as in part a meditation on the myriad factors fuelling our climate crisis (excessive consumption, racism, speciesism). If nothing else, he speaks to how these factors are linked, and in so doing, draws attention (however indirectly or unintended) to the sort of action that needs to be taken in order to avert the environmental apocalypse. We need to 'make kin' as Donna Haraway claims, with and across all manner of others: sexes, races, religions, and species (162; Hudson 685).

If *Mysteries* is best described as developing, through the lens offered by vampire fiction, a hopeful image of what for many is now a goal—namely, a multiculturalism that extends past race to include species—then *True Blood* arguably depicts the obstacles that must be addressed before such a goal can be realised. When seen together in the context of the Anthropocene, *True Blood* and *Mysteries* offer different sides of the same coin, one optimistic, the other more realistic about the ability of humanity to live, eat and act with 'greater moral-ethical response, and responsibility, to non-human life forms' (Nayar 8). It is important to add that optimism is not altogether lost in *True Blood*, which still keeps open the possibility of better relations between humans and vampires. This can be seen, for example, in the last episode of the series, when Hoyt Fortenberry (a human) marries Jessica (a vampire). Although this ceremony is not legally recognised by 'the state of Louisiana [or] the United States of America', as Andy remarks, it is nonetheless a hopeful image, one that is supported by Andy's declaration that 'for my money, there ain't a doubt in my mind that God does [support this union]' ('Thank You' 00:35:06–16). Whether or not it extends to the series as a whole is a matter for another chapter. In any case, it points to a more optimistic trajectory, one that holds the promise for a new multispecies world guided by greater ethical and moral relations between all manners of life forms.

WORKS CITED

Aldana Reyes, Xavier. '"Who Ordered the Hamburger with AIDS?"': Haematophilic Semiotics in *Tru(e) Blood*.' *Gothic Studies*, vol. 15, no. 1, May 2013, pp. 55–65. *Edinburgh UP*, https://doi.org/10.7227/GS.15.1.6.
Alvaro, C. 'Lab-grown Meat and Veganism: A Virtue-oriented Perspective.' *Journal of Agricultural and Environmental Ethics*, vol. 32, no. 1, 2019, pp. 127–41.
Amador, Victoria. 'Blacks and Whites, Trash and Good Country People in *True Blood*.' Cherry, pp. 112–38.
Anyiwo, Melissa. 'Beautifully Broken: *True Blood*'s Tara Thornton as the Black Best Friend.' *Gender in the Vampire Narrative*, edited by Amanda Hobson and U. Melissa Anyiwo, BRILL, 2016, pp. 93–180. *ProQuest Ebook Central*, ebookcentral.proquest.com/lib/unimelb/detail.action?docID=4737016.
Atkinson, Ted. '"Blood Petroleum": *True Blood*, the BP Oil Spill, and Fictions of Energy/Culture.' *Journal of American Studies*, vol. 47, no. 1, Feb. 2013, pp. 213–29. *JSTOR*, www.jstor.org/stable/23352514.
Blayde, Ariadne, and George A. Dunn. 'Pets, Cattle, and Higher Life Forms on *True Blood*.' Irwin et al., pp. 33–48.
Brace, Patricia, and Robert Arp. 'Coming Out of the Coffin and Coming Out of the Closet.' Irwin et al., pp. 93–108.
Carter, Jennifer. 'Dressing Up and Playing Human: Vampire Assimilation in the Human Playground.' Irwin et al., pp. 19–32.
Castricano, Jodey, and Rasmus R. Simonsen, editors. *Critical Perspectives on Veganism*. Palgrave Macmillan, 2016. *Springer Link*, https://doi.org/10.1007/978-3-319-33419-6.
Chaplin, Susan. *The Postmillennial Vampire: Power, Sacrifice and Simulation in True Blood, Twilight and Other Contemporary Narratives*. Palgrave Macmillan, 2017. *Springer Link*, https://doi.org/10.1007/978-3-319-48372-6.
Cherry, Brigid, editor. *True Blood: Investigating Vampires and Southern Gothic*. I.B. Tauris, 2012. *ProQuest Ebook Central*, ebookcentral.proquest.com/lib/unimelb/detail.action?docID=1208981.

Crawford, Joseph. *The Twilight of the Gothic? Vampire Fiction and the Rise of the Paranormal Romance.* Wales UP, 2014. *JSTOR*, www.jstor.org/stable/j. ctt9qhjcp.

'Definition of Veganism.' Vegan Society, www.vegansociety.com/go-vegan/definition-veganism. Accessed 19 June 2019.

Dennis, Simone J., and Alison M. Witchard. 'We Have Never Been Meat (but We Could Be).' *Animals in the Anthropocene: Critical Perspectives on Non-Human Futures,* edited by The Human Animal Research, Sydney UP, 2015, pp. 151–64. *JSTOR*, www.jstor.org/stable/j.ctt1bh4b7h.

Elliot-Smith, Darren. 'Homosexual Vampire as A Metaphor for ... The Homosexual Vampire? *True Blood*, Homonormativity and Assimilation.' Cherry, pp. 139–54.

Gelder, Ken. 'Southern Vampires: Anne Rice, Charlaine Harris and *True Blood.*' *The Palgrave Handbook of Southern Gothic*, edited by Sarah Castillo Street and Charles L. Crow, 2016, pp. 405–19. *Springer Link*, https://doi.org/10.1057/978-1-137-47774-3.

Gerhards, Lea. 'Vampires "On a Special Diet": Identity and the Body in Contemporary Media Texts.' *Dracula and the Gothic in Literature, Pop Culture and the Arts*, edited by Isabel Ermida, BRILL, 2015, pp. 237–58. *ProQuest Ebook Central*, ebookcentral.proquest.com/lib/unimelb/detail.action?docID=4007474.

Haraway, Donna. 'Anthropocene, Capitalocene, Plantationocene, Chthulucene: Making Kin.' *Environmental Humanities*, vol. 6, no.1, 2015, pp. 159–65, environmentalhumanities.org/arch/vol6/6.7.pdf.

Harrington, Nancy, and Alan Ball. 'Excerpt from Interview with Alan Ball: *True Blood* and Beyond.' *Alan Ball: Conversations*, edited by Thomas Fahy, Mississippi UP, 2013, pp. 105–14. *JSTOR*, www.jstor.org/stable/j.ctt2tvnht.

Harris, Charlaine. *All Together Dead.* 2007. Gollancz, 2009.
———. *Club Dead.* 2003. Gollancz, 2009.
———. *Dead and Gone.* 2009. Gollancz, 2010.
———. *Dead as a Doornail.* 2005. Gollancz, 2009.
———. *Dead Ever After.* Gollancz, 2013.
———. *Dead in the Family.* Gollancz, 2010.
———. *Deadlocked.* Gollancz, 2012.
———. *Dead to the World.* 2004. Gollancz 2009.
———. *Dead Until Dark.* 2001. Gollancz, 2009.
———. *Definitely Dead.* 2006. Gollancz, 2009.
———. *Living Dead In Dallas.* 2002. Gollancz, 2009.

Hopkins, Patrick D., and Austin Dacey. 'Vegetarian Meat: Could Technology Save Animals and Satisfy Meat Eaters?' *Journal of Agricultural and Environmental Ethics*, vol. 21, no. 6, pp. 579–96. *Springer Link*, https://doi.org/10.1007/s10806-008-9110-0.

Hudson, Dale. "'Of Course There Are Werewolves and Vampires'": *True Blood* and the Right to Rights for Other Species.' *Species/Race/Sex*, special issue of *American Quarterly*, edited by Sarah Banet-Weiser, vol. 65, no. 3, Sept. 2013, pp. 661–87. *JSTOR*, www.jstor.org/stable/43822924.

Hughes, James. 'Posthumans and Democracy in Popular Culture.' *The Palgrave Handbook of Posthumanism in Film and Television*, edited by Michael Hauskeller et al., Palgrave Macmillan, 2015, pp. 235–45. *Springer Link*, https://doi.org/10.1057/9781137430328.

Irwin, William, George A. Dunn, and Rebecca Housel, editors. *True Blood and Philosophy: We Wanna Think Bad Things with You.* Wiley, 2010.

Johnson, Ayana Elizabeth. 'I'm a Black Climate Expert. Racism Derails Our Efforts to Save the Planet.' *The Washington Post*, June 3, 2020, www.washingtonpost.com/outlook/2020/06/03/im-black-climate-scientist-racism-derails-our-efforts-save-planet/. Accessed 5 June 2020.

Kendi, Ibram X. *Stamped from The Beginning: A Definitive History of Racist Ideas in America.* Bold Type Books, 2017.

Levina, Marina. *Pandemics and the Media.* Peter Lang, 2015.

Lynch, John, and Raymond Pierrehumbert. 'Climate Impacts of Cultured Meat and Beef Cattle.' *Frontiers in Sustainable Food Systems*, vol. 3, Feb. 2019, pp. 1–11, https://doi.org/10.3389/fsufs.2019.00005.

Mallet, Marie-Louise, editor. 'The Animal That Therefore I Am (More to Follow).' *The Animal That Therefore I Am*, by Jacques Derrida and David Wills, Fordham UP, 2008, pp. 1–51. *JSTOR*, www.jstor.org/stable/j.ctt13x09fn.

Mansbridge, Joanna. 'Endangered Vampires of the Anthropocene: Jim Jarmusch's *Only Lovers Left Alive* and the Ecology of Romance.' *Genre: Forms of Discourse and Culture*, vol. 53, no. 2, Dec. 2019, pp. 207–28. *Duke UP*, https://doi-org.eu1.proxy.openathens.net/10.1215/00166928-7965805.

Marrati, Paola. 'True Blood, Bon Temps, Louisiana 2008–2012.' *Philosophy and New American TV Series*, special issue of *MLN*, edited by Paola Marrati and Martin Shuster, vol. 127, no. 5, Dec. 2012, pp. 981–96. *JSTOR*, www.jstor.org/stable/43611277.

McClelland, Bruce. 'Un-True Blood: The Politics of Artificiality.' Irwin et al., pp. 79–90.

McGregor, Andrew, and Donna Houston. 'Cattle in the Anthropocene: Four Propositions.' *Transactions of the Institute of British Geographers*, vol. 43, no. 1, Mar. 2018, pp. 3–16. *Wiley Online Library*, https://doi.org/10.1111/tran.12193.

McFarland-Taylor, Sarah. *Ecopiety: Green Media and the Dilemma of Environmental Virtue.* NYU Press, 2019.

Metcalf, Jacob. 'Meet Schmeat: Food System Ethics, Biotechnology and Re-Worlding Technoscience.' *Parallax*, vol. 19, no. 1, 2013, pp. 74–87, https://doi.org/10.1080/13534645.2013.743294.

Miller, John. 'In Vitro Meat: Power, Authenticity and Vegetarianism.' *Journal for Critical Animal Studies*, vol. 10, no. 4, 2012, pp. 41–63, www.criticalanimal-studies.org/wp-content/uploads/2012/12/JCAS-Volume-10-Issue-4-2012.pdf.

Mutch, Deborah. 'Coming Out of the Coffin: The Vampire and Transnationalism in the *Twilight* and Sookie Stackhouse Series.' *Critical Survey*, vol. 23, no. 2, 2011, pp. 75–90. *Berghahn Journals*, https://doi.org/10.3167/cs.2011.230206.

Ní Fhlainn, Sorcha. *Postmodern Vampires: Film, Fiction, and Popular Culture.* Palgrave Macmillan, 2019. *Springer Link*, https://doi.org/10.1057/978-1-137-58377-2.

Paquet-Deyris, Anne-Marie. 'Alan Ball's California and Louisiana Series, Six Feet Under and True Blood: A Troubled State of the Nation.' *TV/SERIES*, vol. 1, 2012, pp. 188–208. *Open Edition*, https://doi.org/10.4000/tvseries.1195.

Poirier, Nathan, and Joshua Russell. 'Does In Vitro Meat Constitute Animal Liberation?' *Journal of Animal Ethics*, vol. 9, no. 2, fall 2019, pp. 199–211. *JSTOR*, https://doi.org/10.5406/janimalethics.9.2.0199.

Polish, Jennifer. 'Decolonizing Veganism: On Resisting Vegan Whiteness and Racism.' Castricano and Simonsen, pp. 373–91.

Quinn, Emelia, and Ben Westwood. Introduction. 'Thinking Through Veganism.' *Thinking Veganism in Literature and Culture*, edited by Emelia Quinn and Ben Westwood, Palgrave Macmillan, 2018, pp. 1–24. *Springer Link*, https://doi.org/10.1007/978-3-319-73380-7.

Rabin, Nicole. 'True Blood: The Vampire as a Multicultural Critique on Post-race Ideology.' *Journal of Dracula Studies*, vol. 12, 2010, https://research.library.kutztown.edu/dracula-studies/vol12/iss1/4/.

Rowley, Jeanette. 'Human Rights Are Animal Rights: The Implications of Ethical Veganism for Human Rights.' Castricano and Simonsen, pp. 67–92.

Smith, Michelle J. 'The Postmodern Vampire in "Post-race" America: HBO's *True Blood*.' *Open Graves, Open Minds: Representations of the Vampire and the Undead from the Enlightenment to the Present Day*, edited by Sam George and Bill Hughes, Manchester UP, 2013, pp. 192–209. *JSTOR*, www.jstor.org/stable/j.ctt18mvm36.

Spencer, Collin. *The Heretics Feast: A History of Vegetarianism.* Fourth Estate, 1993.

Stephanou, Aspasia. 'A "Ghastly Operation": Transfusing Blood, Science, and the Supernatural in Vampire Texts.' *Gothic Studies*, vol. 15, no. 2, Nov. 2013, pp. 53–65. *Edinburgh UP*, https://doi.org/10.7227/GS.15.2.4.

———. *Reading Vampire Gothic Through Blood: Bloodlines.* Palgrave Macmillan, 2014. *ProQuest Ebook Central*, ebookcentral.proquest.com/lib/unimelb/detail.action?docID=1765631.

Stevenson, John Allen. 'A Vampire in the Mirror: The Sexuality of Dracula.' *PMLA*, vol. 103, no. 2, Mar. 1988, pp. 139–49. *JSTOR*, www.jstor.org/stable/462430.

Wetmore, Kevin J. 'The War on Terror (and Werewolves): Post-9/11 Horror and the Gothic Clash of Civilisations.' *Gothic Studies*, vol. 17, no. 2, Nov 2015, pp. 57–68. *Edinburgh UP*, https://doi.org/10.7227/GS.17.2.4

Woolfork, Lisa. 'I Want to Do Bad Things with You: HBO's *True Blood*'s Racial Allegories in a Post-racial South.' *The South Carolina Review*, vol. 47, no. 2, 2015, pp. 111–32.

Wright, Laura. *The Vegan Studies Project: Food, Animals, and Gender in the Age of Terror*. Georgia UP, 2015. *JSTOR*, www.jstor.org/stable/j.ctt183q3vb.

TV

'Burning House of Love.' Directed by Marcos Siega. *True Blood*, season 1, episode 7, HBO, 19 Oct. 2008. *Binge*, https://binge.com.au/.

'Don't You Feel Me.' Directed by Howard Deutch. *True Blood*, season 6, episode 6, HBO, 21 July 2013. *Binge*, https://binge.com.au/.

'Everybody Wants to Rule the World.' Directed by Daniel Attias. *True Blood*, season 5, episode 9, HBO, 5 Aug. 2012. *Binge*, https://binge.com.au/.

'Everything is Broken.' Directed by Scott Winant. *True Blood*, season 3, episode 9, HBO, 15 Aug. 2010. *Binge*, https://binge.com.au/.

'Gone, Gone, Gone.' Directed by Scott Winant. *True Blood*, season 5, episode 10, HBO, 12 Aug. 2010. *Binge*, https://binge.com.au/.

'Hopeless.' Directed by Daniel Attias. *True Blood*, season 5, episode 6, 15 July HBO, 2010. *Binge*, https://binge.com.au/.

'I Don't Wanna Know.' Directed by Scott Winant. *True Blood*, season 1, episode 10, HBO, 9 Nov. 2008. *Binge*, https://binge.com.au/.

'I Got a Right to Sing the Blues.' Directed by Michael Lehmann. *True Blood*, season 3, episode 6, HBO, 25 July 2010. *Binge*, https://binge.com.au/.

'In the Beginning.' Directed by Michael Ruscio. *True Blood*, season 5, episode 7, HBO, 22 July 2012. *Binge*, https://binge.com.au/.

'9 Crimes.' Directed by David Petrarca. *True Blood*, season 3, episode 4, HBO, 11 July 2010. *Binge*, https://binge.com.au/.

'Plaisir d'Amour.' Directed by Anthony M. Hemingway. *True Blood*, season 1, episode 9, HBO, 2 Nov. 2008. *Binge*, https://binge.com.au/.

'Scratches.' Directed by Scott Winant. *True Blood*, season 2, episode 3, HBO, 28 June 2009. *Binge*, https://binge.com.au/.

'Strange Love.' Directed by Alan Ball. *True Blood*, season 1, episode, 1, HBO, 7 Sept. 2008. *Binge*, https://binge.com.au/.

'The Sun.' Directed by Daniel Attias. *True Blood*, season 6, episode 2, HBO, 23 June 2013. *Binge*, https://binge.com.au/.

'Sunset.' Directed by Lesli Linka Glatter. *True Blood*, season 5, episode 11, HBO, 19 Aug. 2012. *Binge*, https://binge.com.au/.

'Thank You.' Directed by Alan Ball. *True Blood*, season 7, episode 10, HBO, 24 Aug. 2014. *Binge*, https://binge.com.au/.

'To Love is to Bury.' Directed by Nancy Oliver. *True Blood*, season 1, episode 11, HBO, 16 Nov. 2008. *Binge*, https://binge.com.au/.

'You'll Be the Death of Me.' Directed by Alan Ball. *True Blood*, season 1, episode, 12, HBO, 23 Nov. 2008. *Binge*, https://binge.com.au/.

CHAPTER 7

Conclusion: Vampires in the Anthropocene and Beyond

Abstract This chapter summarises the key reasons for the shift in the diet of (some) vampires, from human to animal or synthetic blood, or to human blood that has been given freely, explored throughout this volume and in so doing makes a case for reading these texts through the lens of vegetarianism. It then addresses the recent surge or, perhaps, the resurgence of texts in which the vampire's monstrous thirst for human blood is not diminished. It argues that this strand of the vampire story, at the point of feeding, complements rather than dispatches the developments and concerns of the vegetarian vampire. The chapter then ends by showing how, in both of its incarnations (as a vegetarian or as a virus), the contemporary vampire articulates, albeit in different ways, the concerns aroused by the Anthropocene.

Keywords Vegetarian • Virus • Vampire • Anthropocene • COVID-19

This book has mapped the emergence and gradual development of the vegetarian vampire, as seen in representative examples of late-twentieth and twenty-first-century vampire texts. Its central argument has been that the shift in the diet of (some) vampires, from human to animal or synthetic blood, or from human blood that has been given freely, is in large part a response to a growing ecological awareness to do with species relations. It has shown some of the ways in which the vampire's transition from a diet of human to animal, synthetic or donated human blood can be related to the concerns raised and questions posed by the Anthropocene, which centre on the need to eat, live, and act in ways that are sustainable, do no harm to the environment, and are informed by an ethic of care and responsibility for other species. Regarding the last of these points, this book linked the diverse blood diets now available to vampires, and their newfound ability to choose between diets of human and animal or synthetic blood, with the challenges of ethical consumption, while also exploring the multitude of human-vampire relations that are opened when the 'other' (humans for vampires; animals for humans) is no longer a source of food. In these texts, (some) vampires emerge as helpers and protectors of humanity, with the capacity to become fellow citizens, friends, and even lovers and family to the humans they meet.

As this book has argued, the possibilities introduced by and complications attendant on these relations between species (humans and vampires) are the chief concerns of these vampire texts. Indeed, when one reads or watches, in chronological sequence, *Interview*, *Buffy*, *Twilight*, *The Vampire Diaries* and *True Blood*—and the works on which the fourth and fifth are based, L.J. Smith's *The Vampire Diaries* and Charlaine Harris's *The Southern Vampire Mysteries*—one can trace a growing interest in negotiating and overcoming the species barriers and boundaries that divide humans from vampires. What these texts imagine, in other words, is a world in which humans can live peacefully with their others, with vampire, nonhuman and inhuman forms of life. In each of the texts considered in this book, it is a change in the vampire's diet that enables this more diverse and inclusive world to be imagined.

Conventional understandings read the vampire's changing diet as a continuation of the sympathetic vampire developed in the late-twentieth century, a metaphor for addiction or aspects of capitalism. In previous chapters, I have reframed these arguments to show they have been unable to recognize both the narrowing gap between humans and vampires and these texts' engagement with the changing social and environmental conditions of the Anthropocene. Conventional understandings of the vampire's eating habits do not adequately deal with diet as a vehicle for enabling inter-species relations that are not the norm, something that becomes visible when one looks at these fictions through the lens of vegetarianism.

Finally, the book has suggested that relations between humans and vampires in these texts can be seen as an analogy for relations between humans and animals, and humans and the earth. In many of these texts, good feeding practices, guided by moral, ethical and environmental concerns, lead vampires to seek progressively better, more sustainable ways of feeding and refract growing concerns regarding how humans should live in the Anthropocene. Through these feeding practices, we can begin to explore (albeit at a distance and in fictional form) changes in our own interactions with other humans, animals and the environment that is invited in Anthropocene discourse. At the same time, we also encounter the truth that '[vampires] can be everything we are, while at the same time, they are fearful reminders of the infinite things we are not' (Auerbach 6), a point best conveyed by *True Blood*. In order to make the changes made urgent by the conditions of the Anthropocene, we must address the intersecting sociocultural and political factors fuelling our climate crisis.

As noted in the Introduction, the focus of this book has limited its ability to consider all vampire texts in which animal, donated human or synthetic blood diets appear. Further, it has been unable adequately to address the recent surge or, perhaps, resurgence of horror texts in which the vampire's monstrous thirst for human blood was not diluted. Although this strand of vampire narrative might at first seem disconnected from my argument, it can be argued that, at the point of feeding, it complements the developments and concerns of the vegetarian vampire.

Broadly speaking, vampiric diets in the twenty-first century, whether in their positive (vegetarian) or negative (human-blood-drinking) forms, speak to the concerns of the Anthropocene. In the latter, as seen in literary and cinematic productions like Guillermo del Toro and Chuck Hogan's *The Strain* trilogy (2009–11), later adapted for television (2014–17), *I am Legend* (2007), *Daybreakers* (2009), *Thirst* (2009), *Stakeland* (2010) and, more recently, in *V Wars* (2019) and *The Passage* (2019), adapted from Justin Cronin's novel of the same name (2010), the vampire is linked to fears of viral contagion, voracious consumption and biothreats—fears that are extremely pertinent for our current times, where the threat of COVID-19 seems omnipresent. These fears are linked to the vampire's feeding practices, which in these texts are the vehicles of contagion; but they can also be linked to the collapse of the boundaries that have traditionally divided self and other, human and nonhuman, nature and culture. All these boundaries are contested by the act of vampiric eating or rather drinking. In other words, this strand of the vampire narrative can be seen as anxious about and responsive to our growing awareness of how interconnected and enmeshed we are with nonhuman and inhuman life forms.

This awareness has, of course, been intensified in recent months owing to the COVID-19 epidemic, which draws attention to the links between human and animal life, disease, and death.

In both of its incarnations (as a vegetarian or as a virus), the contemporary vampire articulates, albeit in different ways, the concerns aroused by the Anthropocene. The vampire as a virus can be seen as a troubling echo of our current times, evoking in fictional form the disaster in store if we are unable to adopt more mindful eating practices and the growing recognition that the boundary between humans and animals is not as impermeable as was once thought.[1] As I have argued in this book, the vegetarian vampire speaks to the need to extend 'traditional concepts of ethics, care, and virtue' (Biermann and Lövbrand 2) to animals and the earth—a need that becomes all the more poignant when, looking at contemporary vampire texts as a whole, it emerges in contrast with the alternative represented by the vampire as a virus. As Nina Auerbach claims, each generation of vampires 'feeds on his age distinctively because he embodies that age' (1). But in the works we have been considering, it is *how* the vampire feeds that speaks to the social and environmental conditions of our own times.

WORKS CITED

Auerbach, Nina. *Our Vampires, Ourselves.* Chicago UP, 1995.
Bacon, Simon. *Eco-Vampires: The Undead and the Environment.* McFarland, 2020.
Biermann, Frank, and Eva Lövbrand. Introduction. 'Encountering the Anthropocene: Setting the Scene.' *Anthropocene Encounters: New Directions in Green Political Thinking*, edited by Frank Biermann and Eva Lövbrand, Cambridge UP, 2019, pp. 1–22. *Cambridge Core*, https://doi.org/10.1017/9781108646673.
Del Toro, Guillermo, and Chuck Hogan. *The Strain.* William Morrow, 2009.
———. *The Fall.* William Morrow, 2010.
———. *The Night Eternal.* William Morrow, 2011.
Dungan, Sophie. 'Anthropocene Disease and the Undead in *V Wars*.' *Aeternum: The Journal of Contemporary Gothic Studies*, vol. 8, no. 2, Dec. 2021, pp. 17–33.

[1] For further discussion of how contemporary works that feature the vampire as a virus reflect concerns aroused by the Anthropocene, see Bacon 83–117 and Dungan.

Film and TV

Daybreakers. Directed by Michael Spierig and Peter Spierig, Lionsgate, 2009.
I Am Legend. Directed by Francis Lawrence, Warner Bros. Pictures, 2007.
The Passage. Created by Liz Heldins, Fox, 2019.
The Strain. Created by Guillermo del Toro and Chuck Hogan, FX, 2014–17.
Stakeland. Directed by Jim Mickle, Dark Sky Films / IFC Films, 2010.
Thirst. Directed by Park Chan-woo, Focus Features, 2009.
V Wars. Created by William Laurin and Glenn Davis, Netflix, 2019.

Index[1]

A

Abbott, Stacey, 3n4, 4, 5, 40,
    41n3, 48
African Americans, 78n1, 89, 98, 113
AIDS, 5
The Amazon, 7
American Red Cross, 88, 89n16
Angel, 30, 39–44, 41n3, 42n4, 46–49,
    51, 59, 60
    as Angelus, 41–43, 41n3, 42n4, 45,
        45n9, 64
Angel (TV series), 40, 41n3
Animal-blood diet, 2–6, 3n3, 9, 12,
    13, 24–31, 40–46, 58–60, 62, 68,
    69n14, 77, 78, 80–84, 88, 90,
    91, 98, 101, 104, 123, 125
    and environmental sustainability, 13,
        62–64, 80
    and ethics, 31, 62, 85, 87
    and friendship, 44, 46, 47, 80

good vampire/bad vampire
    dichotomy, 27, 28, 32, 35, 42,
    43, 59, 60, 80, 85
    and impotence, 40–42
    and love, 29, 31, 43–46, 58, 81
    as a metaphor for addiction, 6, 24,
        61, 78n2, 124
    as a metaphor for eating
        disorders, 24, 61
    and morality, 28, 43, 84–87
    and necessity, 29, 44
    as nutritionally inferior and/or
        unsatisfying, 40, 59, 60
    and redemption and/or salvation,
        44, 45, 65, 66
Anthropocene, 3n3, 7–9, 9n9, 12–14,
    62, 64–67, 77, 78, 80, 81,
    85–87, 91, 113, 115,
    124–126, 126n1
race and racial issues, 115

---

[1] Note: Page numbers followed by 'n' refer to notes.